Antoine Laurain lives in Paris. His award-winning novels have been translated into 14 languages and have sold more than 150,000 copies in English. *The President's Hat* was a Waterstones Book Club and Indies Introduce selection, and *The Red Notebook* was on the Indie Next list.

Jane Aitken is a publisher and translator from the French.

Emily Boyce is an editor and in-house translator at Gallic Books.

Praise for *Smoking Kills*:

'Funny, superbly over-the-top . . . not a page too much'
The Times

'*Formidable* – and essential packing for any French summer holiday' *Daily Mail*

'A brisk black comedy . . . Laurain's considered tale retains an elegant detachment . . . And it does, fittingly, make cigarettes seem seductive again, even to committed non-smokers'
The Observer

Praise for *The Portrait*:

'A delightful literary soufflé that fans of his other charming books will savor' *Library Journal*

Praise for *French Rhapsody*:

'Beautifully written, superbly plotted and with a brilliant twist at the end' *Daily Mail*

'The novel has Laurain's signature charm, but with the added edge of greater engagement with contemporary France'
The Sunday Times

Praise for *The Red Notebook*:

'This is in equal parts an offbeat romance, detective story and a clarion call for metropolitans to look after their neighbours

'. . . Reading *The Red Notebook* is a little like finding a gem among the bric-a-brac in a local brocante' *The Telegraph*

'Resist this novel if you can; it's the very quintessence of French romance' *The Times*

'Soaked in Parisian atmosphere, this lovely, clever, funny novel will have you rushing to the Eurostar post-haste . . . A gem' *Daily Mail*

'An endearing love story written in beautifully poetic prose. It is an enthralling mystery about chasing the unknown, the nostalgia for what could have been, and most importantly, the persistence of curiosity' *San Francisco Book Review*

Praise for *The President's Hat*:

'A hymn to *la vie Parisienne* . . . enjoy it for its fabulistic narrative, and the way it teeters pleasantly on the edge of Gallic whimsy' *The Guardian*

'Flawless . . . a funny, clever, feel-good social satire with the page-turning quality of a great detective novel' Rosie Goldsmith

'A fable of romance and redemption' *The Telegraph*

'Part eccentric romance, part detective story . . . this book makes perfect holiday reading' *The Lady*

'Its gentle satirical humor reminded me of Jacques Tati's classic films, and, no, you don't have to know French politics to enjoy this novel' *Library Journal*

Vintage 1954

ANTOINE LAURAIN

Also by Antoine Laurain:

Smoking Kills
The Portrait
French Rhapsody
The Red Notebook
The President's Hat

Vintage 1954

ANTOINE LAURAIN

Translated by Gallic Books
(Jane Aitken/Emily Boyce)

Gallic Books
London

A Gallic Book

First published in France as *Millésime 54*
by Flammarion, 2018
Copyright © Flammarion, Paris, 2018

English translation copyright © Gallic Books, 2019
First published in Great Britain in 2019 by
Gallic Books, 59 Ebury Street,
London, SW1W 0NZ

A CIP record for this book is available from the British Library
ISBN 9781910477670

Typeset in Fournier MT Pro by Palimpsest Book Production Ltd, Falkirk,
Stirlingshire

Printed in the UK by CPI (CR0 4YY)

2 4 6 8 10 9 7 5 3 1

'I'm looking for somewhere else, but a somewhere not far from here'

Jean-Jacques Sempé, *Quelques mystiques*

It happened in the middle of a brightly moonlit night in the Beaujolais vineyards. The official account ran over four typed pages in triplicate:

Charmally-les-Vignes. Monsieur Pierre Chauveau (47) — witness statement on the events of 16 September 1954.
Section 557: local matters

I was going home through the vineyards, a little before midnight. I'd had a drink with Michel Perigot and François Lecharny at L'Auberge de la Belette Rouge, and then I'd left them at the war memorial. Anyway . . . I was making my way through the vineyards with only the moon to guide me. It wasn't giving off much light, but it didn't matter, I know the way like the back of my hand. Nothing seemed out of the ordinary. That's when it happened (WITNESS PAUSES). There was a very bright flash, like the moment lightning strikes, except that this lasted for a while. I was in the Saint-Antoine vineyard, the one Jules Beauchamps owns. The flash was huge, and there were lights everywhere in the sky. It looked like a town with lots of tiny little windows, but there was no sound. I couldn't believe what I was seeing. I felt so dizzy I had to sit down in the dirt. The thing stayed there for a while, hovering over the vines. Perhaps there were people in it looking down at me. Then suddenly it vanished as quickly as it had appeared. But it was there. I saw it and that's why I've come to give a statement even though my wife and family advised me not to. I've come to report what I saw to the authorities.

> Being of sound mind and body
> and in full possession of my faculties,
> Pierre Chauveau

This unusual testimony was classified by the police as follows: Report of an unidentified flying object by one Pierre Chauveau, a winegrower residing in Charmally-les-Vignes. Despite the singular nature of the account, the duty officers that morning were not overly surprised. Since the beginning of the year police stations across the country had taken down an unusually high number of such statements. Coming from all walks of life, the witnesses included notorious alcoholics, storytellers, lawyers, the simple-minded, local notables, unknown truck drivers, priests, city-dwellers and farmers. The police did their job and duly noted down people's accounts, passed them on to the relevant authority and filed them away in triplicate. The press – especially the local papers – never passed up an opportunity to entertain readers with these bizarre tales. By the end of 1954, more than a thousand witness statements and almost five hundred reports of UFO sightings had been received by the police across the country. No explanation for this phenomenon was ever found, and gradually the number of reported sightings fell back to normal levels – between fifty and a hundred a year.

As his family had predicted, Chauveau was endlessly mocked, and he earned the nickname of 'Mr Flying Saucer'.

In 1978, his grandchildren took him to see *Close Encounters of the Third Kind*. When the mother ship appeared on screen to the amazement of François Truffaut in the role of Claude Lacombe, Pierre Chauveau shouted, 'That's the one I saw! I saw the whole thing in 1954!' The other cinema goers tutted and shushed, and one, who could not be identified, called out, 'Shut up, Chauveau!' That evening at dinner, as his wife looked on disapprovingly, Pierre Chauveau decided to drink the bottle of Château Saint-Antoine 1954 that he had laid down. As usual, he also poured a drop into the bowl of his dog, Ausweis – daughter of Schnell, granddaughter of Sieg, a German shepherd left behind by the Waffen SS as they fled, whom everyone assumed was part wolf.

The next day, he set off for the wine cooperative and neither he nor Ausweis was ever seen again. The last image his nearest and dearest would have of him was of a man with his dog at his side, raising his collar and drawing on his pipe: 'Foul weather,' he had said, then he had closed the door and never reappeared. His family had put out a missing person appeal, dragged the ponds and organised a search of the forests but all to no avail.

The wine produced by the Saint-Antoine vineyard in 1954 had been exceptional. The eight hundred bottles of that vintage were all snapped up that year. Even though the wine was new it seemed to have the depth of flavour of a thirty-year-old *grand cru*. An oenologist declared that he detected 'the tannic notes and lingering flavour of a very good Chambolle-Musigny'. Jules Beauchamps said that was because of his hard work and the new techniques he had used. But he was never able to reproduce such wonderful wine and Château Saint-Antoine reverted to being the very ordinary table wine it had always been.

'Please fasten your seat belts, stow your tray tables and return your seats to the upright position. We are now beginning our descent into Roissy-Charles-de-Gaulle. The local time is nineteen forty, and the temperature on the ground is fourteen degrees.' By the time the announcement had been made the powerful landing gear of the American Airlines Boeing 767 had already locked into place. Paris. Finally. After the ten-hour flight, Bob Brown would set foot in Paris for the first time in his life. He closed the copy of Hemingway's *A Moveable Feast* given to him by his son and daughter, folded his table away and moved his seat into the upright position. 'Here we go, Goldie . . .' Bob murmured, tapping the armrest of the empty seat next to him. On the aisle side of him, a fat Chinese man dozed on, his sleep mask over his eyes. The air hostess gently woke him, whereupon he in turn put the back of his seat up.

Bob and his wife Goldie had always dreamed of going to Paris. As the years had gone by, the French capital had taken on mythical status. Montmartre, the Eiffel Tower, Notre Dame, the bridges of the Seine, Place de la Concorde, the Louvre, café terraces, the Opéra and other well-known landmarks seemed to belong to an enchanted city that would be forever out of their reach. Like ancient Alexandria with its lighthouse and library, the Colossus of Rhodes, or the Hanging Gardens of Babylon, with its trees and flowers cascading in tiers towards the Euphrates. Their obsession with Paris dated back to when they first met.

Thirty years earlier, aged twenty-eight, Bob had pushed through the saloon doors of Why Not, a bar on Lyon Street in Milwaukee. That stifling August day, he was due to meet another young man who was selling a second-hand Harley-Davidson XR-750. It wasn't in great shape, but the price was enticing. Because he was a mechanic, Bob wanted to see the bike before making an offer with the few hundred dollars he had set aside. He had gone up to the bar, and come upon the blonde hair and pretty smile of Goldie Delphy, the new barmaid who was wiping pint glasses with her delicate hands. Years later Goldie would often describe this scene to their children: 'Your father came into my bar like Clint Eastwood!' To which Bob would always add, 'I'd only ever seen women like your mother on garage calendars!'

The meeting to buy the Harley would have to wait. Because now Bob could only think about the barmaid and the Milwaukee-made motorbike no longer seemed important. But how to approach her without sounding like an idiot or creep or, most likely, both? Bob's eye was caught by a postcard of the Eiffel Tower against a blue sky, sellotaped to the pillar of the bar. He thought he might try saying 'Eiffel Tower' in French and smiling at the young woman. That might work. It would sound intelligent, worldly, perhaps. He sipped his beer and launched in with '*Le Tour Eiffel* . . . Paris!' Goldie immediately turned to him – she too had been wondering for the last quarter of an hour how she could strike up a conversation with Clint Eastwood without sounding like a cheap hooker.

'Yes!' she said enthusiastically. 'It's from a customer who's on holiday over there. He sent it to the owner.'

'It looks cool – so tall!' replied Bob, staring at the image.

'It certainly is. It's as tall as the John Hancock Center in Chicago.' Goldie moved towards Bob to take a closer look at the postcard, though she was very familiar with it by now.

Bob nodded. 'But no one lives inside it?'

'No, it's open to visitors, though.'

'So it's not used for anything?'

'No, nothing at all; they built it because . . . well, just because it's beautiful.'

'What a nation,' said Bob, admiringly, nodding again. 'They assembled thousands of steel girders which weigh a ton, to make a giant pointed thing that does absolutely nothing.'

'Yes,' replied Goldie, 'I think that's very French.' And their faces were even closer together now as they both looked at the monument, as if expecting to see tourists waving back at them.

Bob's meeting never took place. After half an hour talking about people who build useless things, and another half-hour discussing Paris, where neither of them had been, Bob left with Goldie's parents' phone number. He had given her the number of Joe Feldman's garage, Mensch's Motors.

Paris was destined to remain a fantasy for them. Two months after they met, although they had become engaged, chosen their wedding rings and dreamed of spending their honeymoon wandering the streets of Montmartre, Bob was contacted by Harley-Davidson. Their headhunters had spotted his talent as a mechanic, and they were offering him a job designing new engines, for three times what he was earning at Mensch's Motors. Bob's career was taking off and the flight to Paris could not compete.

Over the next thirty years together, Bob and Goldie lived in a lovely house in Milwaukee with a Stars and Stripes flag planted in the garden and brought up two children, Jenny and Bob Junior. Goldie had bought the Why Not bar. And when Bob was getting ready to retire from the engine research department, after three decades' loyal service working to improve the *vroom vroom* of the world's most famous motorcycle, Goldie hired a manager to look after the bar. Time had flown by and they had never got round to leaving the confines of the American continent. Miami, New York and Las Vegas were the furthest they had ever travelled. The rest of the time, they enjoyed motorbike trips on over thirty different Harleys. Bob was part of the Road Captain squad and like all members wore the HOG (Harley Owners Group) black leather vest covered in badges. The Milwaukee Harley-Davidson Chapter was not at all like the pugnacious Hell's Angels. Milwaukee Eagles members were peaceable folks who loved their families, friends, barbecues and the gleam of motorcycle chrome.

'Goldie, it's time!' Bob had said eight months ago. Finally, they would go to Paris. They had been taking language classes at the local French Institute and watching the classic French films their teacher, Abigail Doherty, had recommended because the actors' diction was so clear. Bob and Goldie had discovered Jean Gabin, Maurice Chevalier and Fernandel.

And now they were ready. They had booked flights and worked out where they would stay. But that was when Goldie fell ill. Seriously ill. The first treatment she tried was useless. Her leukaemia was incurable. 'Even though the kids are grown up, you should find a new wife,' Goldie told Bob. 'You won't be able to look after yourself.' Bob had said nothing, turning to look unseeingly at the tree outside the hospital window. 'Bob? Are you listening to me? You don't even know how to put the washing machine on!', and the tree had blurred in front of his eyes, which were suddenly blinded by tears.

Goldie had now been in a coma for two months, her nervous system overwhelmed by cancerous cells, and she was on a ventilator. Her condition had stabilised, but the doctors had ruled out any possibility that she would regain consciousness.

Bob had wanted to abandon the trip to Paris, but the airline was uncooperative. The insurance policy they had taken out did not cover one of the travellers falling into a coma. The only valid reasons for cancellation were the death of a passenger or a letter signed by the passenger who had fallen ill. When, finally, the airline saw sense and agreed to reimburse the tickets 'as a gesture of goodwill because of your unfortunate circumstances', Bob changed his mind and said to his children, 'That damned plane is not leaving without me and your mother!' He turned down a refund, even of Goldie's tickets. The seat beside him would remain empty. Bob packed as best he could. He made a list, and carefully folded his leather HOG vest. He had promised the members of the chapter that he would wear it to take a selfie at the Eiffel Tower. His son drove him from Milwaukee to Chicago airport, and his daughter came too to see him off. Bob Junior's pick-up was escorted all the way by twenty Harleys sporting little American and French flags.

When the plane touched down, Bob opened the folder with the details of his rental apartment, chosen by his children on Airbnb: Madame Renard, 18 Rue Edgar-Charellier – 'If anyone asks, say you are one of the American cousins.'

The studio shop on the ground floor of the building was bathed in evening sunshine. Laid out on the table were the 267 china fragments of a statue of Eros, which would have been about three feet tall before having fallen on the marble-tiled floor of a conservatory. Having carefully counted the pieces, Magalie had sorted them into piles by colour. The beautiful nineteenth-century statue had literally exploded when it hit the ground. The owner had done exactly the right thing and swept all the fragments into a cardboard box before hurrying round to Magalie's studio. Most people think that something that has shattered in this way is broken for ever. But that's not true. Unlike living creatures, objects can be put back together. In three months' time, the beautiful Eros would once again take its place among the plants of the conservatory and no one would ever imagine that it had shattered into 267 little pieces on the floor. Of course, it would have to be handled with care, but that would be all. It would be there, reborn, like all the items which had passed through the hands of Magalie Lecœur over the last five years – a glazed earthenware jug, a marble statue, an enamel goblet, a sculpted ivory figure, a china teacup, an opaline vase … 'You're a magician,' her customers often said to Magalie, and, whether they were antique dealers or ordinary members of the public, it was the best compliment they could pay her.

Magalie had studied Restoration and Conservation at the École de Condé and then trained with several studios before setting up on her own at the age of twenty-seven. She had taken over the lease at 18 Rue Edgar-Charellier from the carpet shop. Azar Raffi, who'd had the shop for thirty years, specialised in Persian rugs and was keen to retire. 'No one wants carpets, these days, Mademoiselle. Young people want waxed parquet now. I sold rugs to their parents, and when they inherit them, they bring them back here! I'm quite happy to buy back my rugs, but who can I sell them on to? I'm like a cat chasing its tail. I'm going round in circles in my shop and I've had enough. I'm off.' The shop came with a vast studio on the sixth floor of the building, made by knocking together several maid's rooms. Azar Raffi used it as a stockroom. Magalie did it up and it became her apartment.

The arrival of the restoration specialist in the building did not pass unnoticed. Magalie may have practised an ancient craft, working in the world of fine art and museums, but her appearance was more gothic rock chick, or perhaps Tim Burton movie character. She had several piercings in her left ear, a pale complexion and scarlet lips. Her hair, which was often in pigtails, was artfully tousled. Her wardrobe consisted mainly of skimpy dresses adorned with skull and crossbones, or cats, and she usually wore ankle boots with big chrome buckles. At first the little old ladies who lived in the building were a bit frightened of Magalie, but they had soon taken her to their hearts after she offered to do their shopping, post their letters and even water their plants or feed cats, dogs or canaries when they were away. It was just such a shame, they said to each other, that such a pretty girl would make herself look so ugly.

One morning she stopped the chairman of the building's management committee in the entrance hall. 'Monsieur Larnaudie, can I ask you something?'

'Of course, and if it's about life at number 18, I should be able to help.'

'Yes, it is about that . . .' Magalie looked down at the studded toes of her boots and then up at Monsieur Larnaudie. 'Is it true that everyone in the building calls me Abby?'

At the time, *NCIS* was breaking viewing records every Friday evening. And one of the main characters was Abby, a young forensic scientist at the Naval Criminal Investigative Service who was highly gifted, always cheerful, and dressed like a goth. She spent all her time in her white coat in the lab, listening to techno music as she pieced together fingerprints, microfibres, SIM cards and DNA to help her colleagues solve crimes. Magalie too was in her studio from morning till night, wearing a white coat and listening to unidentifiable music as she carried out repairs with scientific precision. The resemblance, both physical and professional, had not escaped the residents of the building and they had lost no time in dubbing her Abby.

That morning, Hubert Larnaudie began to reply, 'Listen, Abby, I don't know what people in the building say privately . . .' then he stopped in horror and apologised. 'It's not meant in any way to be insulting, Mademoiselle Lecœur,' he went on seriously. 'On the contrary, it's a mark of our great affection for you. Madame Lacaze and Madame Baulieue, our longest-standing residents, can't speak highly enough of you. You've brought new life to that sleepy old shop and you've won over our concierge, Madame Da Silva — which is not easy. Everyone here likes you tremendously, you can be certain of that.'

Magalie nodded in silence and it seemed to Hubert that there might be tears in her eyes.

'Thank you,' she murmured. 'Have a good day, Monsieur Larnaudie.'

If Magalie was a big hit with the old ladies, she had been less successful when it came to men. Her most recent boyfriend had left her, and all Magalie had to relieve her loneliness was broken fragments on which her hands would work their magic. Unfortunately she was unable to cast the same charm on her own life, which seemed to her like a puzzle whose pieces did not fit.

The fragments of statue spread over her work table shook imperceptibly. A week ago, the tunnel-boring machine extending line 14 of the metro, known as Météor, had reached Rue Edgar-Charellier. The enormous machine with its round boring head was operating more than sixty-five feet below ground but for the last forty-eight hours it seemed to be under number 18, because if you looked closely you could detect vibrations. The fragments stopped shaking and the doorbell rang. 'Coming!' cried Magalie.

She sorted one final fragment and went to open the door to a man of about thirty holding a bunch of violets. 'Is it time to go?' she asked before seeing the flowers.

'I found these on the way; they're for you,' said Julien.

'Thank you! Come in and I'll find a vase for them.' Magalie picked up an opaline vase with a chipped neck and a ticket round it.

'Have you been to one of these management committee meetings before?' she asked Julien as she filled the vase at the tap.

'No, never. I've always rented up until now.'

'Well, you'll see, they go on for ever but they can be entertaining. Monsieur Larnaudie looks after everything; he lives for this building. I bet he's going to talk about the broken basement shutters; he's been obsessing about them for three days now . . . They're very pretty, thank you, Julien,' she said, stepping back to admire the little bouquet on the table.

'I wanted to cheer you up,' mumbled Julien.

'Well, you've succeeded!' She smiled. 'Shall we go?'

Julien glanced at Magalie as they walked along the street, not listening to a word of what she was saying about the annual management committee meetings. It had been love at first sight. There was no other way to describe it. Julien remembered the moment he'd met her four months earlier as clearly as if it had just happened. He had been on his way down to put a few things away in the little cellar that had come with the tiny apartment he had bought with a twenty-year mortgage at 1.6 per cent interest. The cellars were the only part of the building that hadn't been renovated since its construction during the Second Empire. Wooden doors that opened with big iron keys, the dirt floor covered in threadbare rugs and the signs ('Coal bunker', 'Roadside window', 'Communal cellar', 'Lift mechanism'), painted on the walls by signwriters who were long dead, were like relics of a lost world.

'Hi, are you the new owner of the ground-floor apartment? I'm Magalie Lecœur, but everyone here calls me Abby because of some stupid American TV series.' His world had tilted on its axis. Her eyes were so green, her lips so red and smiling, her skin so pearly white. When Magalie had put her hand in his to shake it, it was as if a bomb had gone off inside Julien's head. He felt as though he was finally meeting the faceless girl he had seen in his dreams since his teenage years.

Julien was painfully shy around women, and only came into his own with a cocktail shaker in his hand and a barman's white apron tied around his waist. Back at catering college, he had quickly realised that waiting on tables was not for him. 'Madame, Monsieur, may I present the chef's pot-roast duck accompanied by morel ravioli and a white pepper sauce. Bon appétit'; such phrases would not be the soundtrack to his evenings for long. Coming from Beaujolais, he had been brought up to appreciate a fine vintage, and while his parents had since left the family vineyard for the city, they still upheld the tradition of opening a good bottle on the birthdays and special occasions that punctuated their lives.

One day while on a training placement at a provincial four-star hotel, he had been enchanted by the sight of the newly done-up bar. Dozens of bottles lined the shelves, cleverly lit with coloured LED bulbs. There was something soothing about the warm glow of the lights and the big leather armchairs dotted about the room. The painstakingly polished mahogany bar and its gleaming brass fittings were like a runway on which sparkling glasses would touch down, filled with the most sophisticated drinks. Two customers were sitting talking on a sofa while the barman, a slim man with short white hair and half-moon spectacles, was pouring the contents of several bottles into the cocktail shaker: gin, cherry liqueur, cranberry juice, rose liqueur . . . Julien walked towards him, entranced. The barman, whose name, Gérard, was embroidered on his apron in red thread, looked up and peered over his glasses. 'Trainee, are you?' he muttered.

'Yes, Monsieur,' Julien replied.

'In the kitchen?'

'Front of house, Monsieur.'

The barman gave him a pitying look. 'Here behind the bar we're in our own little world.' He picked up the shaker, shook it smoothly over his shoulder and then opened it. The chrome was frosted from the shaken ice and Gérard divided the chilled liquid perfectly between two triangular glasses before garnishing each one with a cherry and a sprig of fresh mint. 'Golden Jaipur. One of my creations,' he said, placing the glasses on a silver tray and carrying them over to his customers.

That was when Julien knew what he wanted to do with his life. Or rather, where he was meant to be, which was behind a bar, with a white apron with his name embroidered on it tied round his waist and a head full of thousands of cocktails ready to mix on demand, when he wasn't inventing his own.

A month later, Monsieur Gérard was writing a letter which began, 'Monsieur Julien Chauveau is by far the most gifted trainee I have encountered in my long career.' After three years at college, he passed his mixology diploma with top marks. The night before he left for London, he invited his brother, sister and parents to join him for a celebratory meal at one of the best traditional *bouchon* restaurants in Lyon. His father raised his glass and said solemnly, 'Your great-grandfather would have been proud.' There was a silence then Julien said, 'I'm sure he's watching us . . . from above.' No one reacted to that except his younger sister, who rolled her eyes. Then they all turned to drinking an excellent Juliénas.

Pierre Chauveau remained the big mystery of the family. Though Julien had been born ten years after his disappearance in 1978, the tale of 'Mr Flying Saucer' had fascinated him since childhood. He was always asking his father and aunt about the night they had been to a screening of Spielberg's film and his great-grandfather had shouted out in the cinema that the mother ship was just like the one he had seen in 1954. Julien had found out all he could about that year, known to enthusiasts as 'The Year of Flying Saucers'. He had gathered an impressive collection of documents on reported UFO sightings, most precious among which was a rare copy of the self-published 1955 cult classic *Alien Visits and Space Phenomena*, in which the author, legendary astronomer Charles Arpajon, argued that there was a link between flying saucers and time travel.

Julien had discovered to his cost that his hobby was an exclusively masculine pursuit. It seemed women did not believe in flying saucers and considered men with an interest in them to be unreliable dreamers and, frankly, rather infantile. When he had brought up his passion for UFO sightings with his few past love interests, he had soon sensed he was on thin ice. These days, he never raised the subject with anyone of the opposite sex, confining himself to chatting to UFO lovers across the globe online. As far as Julien was concerned, his ancestor had experienced something extraordinary, and his subsequent disappearance must surely be linked to what he had seen. But his family didn't believe in Mr Flying Saucer's improbable vision, and blamed it instead on the alcohol he had imbibed with friends at L'Auberge de la Belette Rouge. The statement he had made to the police had only served to make him look ridiculous. As for his disappearance, if there was any mystery surrounding it, the answer surely lay at the bottom of an undragged pond.

All of this was running through Julien's mind as he made

his way to his first management committee meeting. This, and Magalie, whose inky hair was fluttering in the evening breeze. Neither his encyclopedic knowledge of cocktails nor of flying saucers would go any way towards winning her over. Over the past four months, he had often seen her with a pale-eyed blond man whom he had instantly taken against. This was the man who could hold her in his arms, kiss her, take her to the beach for the weekend, walk hand in hand with her along the water's edge as the sun went down before taking her back to a hotel room. It was so unfair. And yet he had to admit there was now a glimmer of hope: for the last three weeks, Julien hadn't seen her with anyone.

When they got to the crossroads, Julien glanced up at the billboards. There was a big advert for 'Heritage Days', starting the following day. Under the slogan 'Tomorrow starts yesterday!', modern modes of urban transport and vintage cars were pictured outside iconic locations such as the Assemblée Nationale and the Élysée Palace, which were having their annual open days, when Parisians and tourists alike could visit buildings usually closed to the public. The RATP always put on treasure hunts for children across the city's transport network, and old buses with rear platforms and metro carriages with wooden seats were brought out of retirement to mark the occasion.

'We could hop on one of those old buses tomorrow,' Julien suggested, pointing to the advert.

'We could . . .' smiled Magalie. 'But it'd be better if they could really take us back in time! I'd have loved to see Les Halles back when it was a real marketplace, with Baltard's glass halls filled with butchers and greengrocers. My grandmother used to talk about it all the time. She said everyone would mingle in the restaurants after hours: butchers, well-heeled diners, American tourists, film stars . . .'

Julien smiled, nodding his head. He could just picture himself sitting at one of those jolly, noisy tables, with dishes of bœuf bourguignon and champagne corks popping all around.

'Watch out!' said Magalie, placing a hand on his forearm. The light had just turned green and a scooter had already zoomed out in front of them.

The touch of her hand made his heart beat faster, but it also brought him back to reality: this was 2017, and no bus was going to take them back to dine in the past.

'I assume that Monsieur Larnaudie will be chairing the meeting as usual,' asked Mademoiselle Prusin in her commanding voice.

The fourteen people around the large meeting table in the managing agent's office nodded.

'Thank you for that vote of confidence,' began Hubert Larnaudie. 'Let's start on the agenda. First of all, I would like to welcome Julien Chauveau, who is new to the building. He has bought the ground-floor flat, on the left-hand side of the courtyard, where Monsieur Bellier used to live. Julien is a barman at the famous Harry's Bar.'

Julien smiled and nodded, catching Magalie's eye. She winked at him.

'I'm sorry not to see Madame Renard here. To my mind, she Airbnbs her apartment far too often. I'm always coming across new people on the stairs dragging suitcases who all assure me they're cousins of Madame Renard. She appears to have cousins of all ages all over the world . . . But we can return to that later. In addition to Madame Renard, Monsieur Mercier and Madame Merlino have also sent their apologies. Let's start by looking at the annual accounts.'

Hubert held the honorary position of chairman of the management committee because of his encyclopedic knowledge of 18 Rue Edgar-Charellier. 'I've lived here since 1868,' he was fond of saying, as if he had defied the laws of time by being remarkably well preserved for a man of 140 and looking only about 50. Hubert always smiled when he said this and what he meant was that it was his family that had built the apartment block during Haussmann's renovation of Paris. Previously, Rue Edgar-Charellier had been nothing but a field containing the remains of Saint-Martin Abbey, which had been destroyed in the French Revolution. Hubert owned a family print entitled *Creation of Rue Edgar-Charellier, 1868*. The print was of a commanding-looking man sitting on a barrel, map in hand, indicating to passers-by where the new street would run. In the distance, workmen were clearing away earth and completing the destruction of the vestiges of the abbey, on the site of which number 18 would be built.

In the glory days of the past, the six-storey building overlooking the street and the five-storey building overlooking the courtyard had been entirely owned by the Larnaudie family. Brothers, sisters, cousins, nephews and grandparents had divided up the floors and the family had rented out the other apartments to the middle classes flocking to the new district. The sixth floor had been allocated to the servants who looked after all the residents. Gradually, as the generations grew up, moved on and married, the Larnaudies had sold off more and more of the apartments. Hubert was always lamenting how little his family had received for these sales. Up until the 1950s the third floor overlooking the courtyard still belonged to them but his grandfather had sold it at a knock-down price after losing all his money in Suez Canal shares. Six generations after the building's construction, all that remained of this splendid heritage was the third floor of the building overlooking the street, one loft and two cellars.

Among the family papers, Hubert still had the original plans to number 18 drawn in ink and signed by Second Empire architects. He knew where all the load-bearing walls were, what the servants' quarters looked like before they were turned into studios, where the old chimneys were located and where the taps used to be. He also knew the names of all the tenants and concierges who had ever occupied the building, having heard his father and uncle referring to them. Even more strikingly, he personally undertook to French polish the lift cabin three times a year. The mechanism of the lift had been entirely updated by now, but the mahogany cabin with its crystal Lalique light and arched glass doors with flower-shaped brass handles remained. It dated from 1911. That year, Anatole Larnaudie, Hubert's great-great-grandfather, the doyen of the building and a cantankerous old man, had decided to modernise the building by installing a lift. The family advised against it. So Anatole had paid for its construction out of his own pocket. The cost had been considerable. However, Anatole got his own back by putting an ironic inscription on the inside of the lift: 'Gift of Anatole Larnaudie, our great benefactor. First five-floor ascent by the grateful owners and tenants achieved 21 September 1911.'

After Hubert had summarised the previous year's accounts and mentioned that the tunnelling for the extension of the metro might cause some cracks to appear in the cellars, he raised a matter that he described as being of the utmost urgency.

The shutters of the communal cellar were broken, and it was essential to get a locksmith as soon as possible, otherwise anyone would be able to get in. There had been some burglaries in the area. 'Gypsies . . .' concluded Hubert, soberly.

'Why do we have shutters there anyway?' asked Monsieur Berthier.

'For the delivery of coal!' replied Hubert as if it were obvious. 'Each cellar used to have a coal hole, and the apartments all had a fireplace in every room.'

The owners nodded, wondering what had become of the fireplaces.

'I'll call TTS Locksmiths tomorrow morning, Monsieur Larnaudie,' said Mademoiselle Prusin. 'Now point 7: general building matters. Madame Merlino, who can't be here but who has authorised Monsieur Larnaudie to act for her, points out that the communal cellar is cluttered with belongings left over the years by various owners. "We could" – I'm quoting Madame Merlino's email – "clear out our own cellars and put everything we don't want to keep into the communal cellar and then get a house-clearance company to come and remove it all." What does everyone think?' asked Mademoiselle Prusin.

Hubert thought about his own two cellars, where a motley jumble of items from a period covering two world wars were all crammed in. He had never seen his father go near them and he had never looked at them himself. Objects were heaped up, forming geological layers, each one representing a different generation. In the old days, you didn't throw things away, you put them in the cellar. And Hubert had continued the habit. He, too, had contributed to the family scrapheap by adding children's bikes, soft toys, games tables, stools, book-cases, a fish tank and record players. Tidying it all up would take a whole tiresome weekend amid dust and spiders' webs, and it would be a melancholy task.

Mog, the family cat, was fast asleep on the living-room radiator, having apparently decided to go into hibernation before winter had even begun. He opened one eye when Hubert entered the room but quickly resumed his feline dreams. Hubert stroked him and received a flick of the tail in return. Sitting alone in his apartment with a glass of whisky, he was mulling over Madame Merlino's proposed cellar clear-out, which the committee had passed without turning a hair, when his phone rang. 'Charlotte', his wife's name, flashed up on screen. It was mid-September and Charlotte was extending the summer holidays with her childhood friend Chantal in their house in Noirmoutier. The two women seemed to be having a whale of a time away from their husbands and children. They had visited an antiques fair and an organic market and were now trying out a fish recipe from an old cookbook they had picked up at one of the stalls.

'You'll cook yourself something tonight, won't you?'

'Yes, yes, of course,' replied Hubert, noting that his wife's question sounded rather like a reproach, or an order to be carried out post haste.

After he had rung off, it occurred to Hubert that he hadn't heard much from his children, Camille and Olivier, since the start of term. Both were now pursuing their studies far from Rue Edgar-Charellier.

He opened the fridge and silently scanned the shelves. He had forgotten to do any shopping and the food that was left looked distinctly uninviting. He closed the door and turned off the kitchen light. He took a bunch of keys and a pocket torch from the drawer in the hallway and slammed the front door behind him.

The door to his cellar opened with an ominous creak. '*Mon Dieu*, it's worse than I remembered.'

The torchlight picked out a jumble of objects piled several feet high, ranging from a chair with an abacus Camille had used as a child, to a French flag from the Liberation of Paris, by way of a handless clock Hubert had never seen in his life and a soldier's helmet dating back to 1914. Hubert cursed his forebears for leaving him to sort out over a hundred years of mess. He groped about for the old inspection light, hung it on the nail and plugged it in just outside the door. Ta dah! Suddenly the pigsty was displayed in all its terrible glory.

'Utter madness . . .' grumbled Hubert as he came upon hundreds of copies of *L'Illustration* from the 1910s.

Why on earth had they kept all these magazines, a single pile of which was as hard to lift as a sleeping Labrador? Could they not have thrown them away after reading them, like everyone else? Fishing rods lay along one wall, veterans of many a happy outing between the wars. His eye passed over black-and-white engravings of chateau life: guests in powdered wigs sitting down to candle-lit dinners, games of blindman's bluff in the gardens. With his suit now flecked with dust, Hubert sneezed, caught his foot in the handle of a shovel lying on the floor and tripped, breaking his fall on a mountain of tin plates, a candelabra, a bedside table, a pulley and several old boxes of books. Lying with his hands flat on the dirt floor, he was about to push himself up when he caught sight of a dusty bottle propped against a pile of rolled-up posters in the corner of the room. Struggling to his feet, Hubert picked up the bottle and held it up to the lamp, which had been swinging slowly since his fall. As he gently brushed off the dust, the glass shone like ink and the label was legible once more: 'Château Saint-Antoine, 1954. Domaine Jules Beauchamps'. Hubert squinted through the glass – the liquid remained clear, crimson reflections glimmering in the lamp light, and had not evaporated, or given up what is poetically known as 'the angel's share'. Just then, he heard a rush of air, the door slamming shut and a key turning in the lock.

Hubert froze. The image of the closed door took a good second and a half to register.

'Hey! What's going on?'

He heard footsteps running down the corridor.

'Hurry up! There's a guy in there; I locked him in. We've gotta get out of here!' he heard in the distance.

'Hey! Who's there? Open up!' shouted Hubert, banging on the door. 'I'm calling the police!'

He reached into his jacket pocket to find he had left his phone on the kitchen table. Perfect. The broken cellar shutters had not gone unnoticed and now here he was locked in while his neighbours had their cellars ransacked.

'I'm calling the police!' he shouted again. 'The station's two streets away!'

He stepped over the family detritus and stood under the ventilation grate that looked onto the courtyard.

'Hello! Is anyone there?' he shouted. 'It's Monsieur

Larnaudie. We're being burgled! I'm locked in my cellar! Madame Da Silva? Maria?'

His cries met with silence. 'For crying out loud, she's gone to eat at her sister's again!' fumed Hubert. As for the residents of the building, they had all closed their windows against the cool September evening and could not hear him.

I'm trapped, thought Hubert. Trapped in a space of a hundred square feet. The thought took shape in his mind. The prospect of spending the night curled up among his family's belongings was becoming a distinct possibility.

The little café was buzzing with conversations at the counter, tinkling cutlery and the whirr of the coffee machine. Bob wheeled his suitcase into L'ESPÉRANCE — CAFÉ — TABAC — PETITE BRASSERIE À TOUTE HEURE and approached the imposing blonde woman at the till.

'*Bonsoir madame, je venir chercher le clefs de Madame Renard.*'

Smiling to herself, the café owner turned to the dark-haired man presiding over the cigarette counter and barked, 'Robert! Where've you put Françoise's keys?'

'In my pocket!'

'What kind of answer is that?'

Robert twisted round to reach into his jeans pocket and pull out in a single handful a hankie, a bunch of keys, a cigarette lighter and a few coins which showered onto the floor. He walked over to his wife, dangling the keys from his fingertips. 'There's your answer, Maryse.'

As he came to number 18, Bob saw a painting in an ornate gilt frame being passed out through a wide cellar window and bundled into a white van by two men who drove off at full speed. Bob watched the van screech down the road before peering through the metal shutters into the cellars, but all he could make out was a wooden stepladder leading down into the darkness. He pushed the shutters to. What he had just witnessed did not look right. In fact, it looked suspiciously like a burglary. He thought about going into the shop at the bottom of the building, A&R ARTS ET RESTAURATION — MAGALIE LECŒUR. The lights were on and through the blinds he could see two figures at the back of the shop. But it was late — what exactly was he going to say to them? He was an American staying in an Airbnb in the building. He would do better to keep a low profile.

Still holding the owner's instructions, he tapped in the door code, entered the building and walked towards the lift. He pressed the button and the cabin came trundling down. Leaving his suitcase in the hall, Bob peered inside. With its precious beeswax-scented wood, little glazed doors, delicate ceiling light and brass flower-shaped handles, the contraption resembled no elevator he had ever seen before. It was as beautiful as a very early Harley. 'Oh . . . my . . . gosh,' he said to himself when he spotted the 1911 inscription describing the lift as a generous gift from Anatole Larnaudie.

'It's Monsieur Larnaudie! I'm trapped! Let me out!' he heard someone say.

For a moment, Bob wondered if jet lag and the effects of the ten-hour flight were catching up with him. Or if Stephen King's novels might in fact have some truth to them.

'Is anyone there? I can hear the lift!'

Bob stepped back, closed the elevator door and looked around. The voice was coming from the courtyard, a space filled with shrubs and greenery. Behind a potted fig tree, he saw light shining through a metal grating at ground level and, through the bars, a man's face. He bent down.

'Hello, Monsieur.'

'And who might you be?' asked Hubert irritably. 'Was it you who locked me in here?'

'No, I'm . . . Madame Renard's cousin,' Bob remembered to say.

'No, you're not,' replied Hubert, 'but I'm pleased to see you, all the same. I'm locked in my own cellar.'

'I see.'

'Did you notice whether the lights were on in the shop to the left of the front door?'

'Yes, they were on.'

'I'm saved,' sighed Hubert. 'We need to fetch Abby. Go and knock on the window and tell her that Monsieur Larnaudie is locked in his cellar.'

'OK. Abby, Larnaudie . . . cellar. I'll be right back,' said Bob, heading off towards the shop.

'You're very kind, Monsieur,' Hubert called after him from his prison.

Bob rapped on the door of the shop. Behind the blinds, one of the figures moved and came to let him in.

'Oh!' Bob said with a start. 'I can see why he calls you Abby!'

'Excuse me?'

'Thank you all, thank you! What would I have done without you?' said Hubert, dusting himself off in front of Magalie, Julien and Bob. 'I really thought I'd have to spend the night in there.'

'Bob Brown, from Milwaukee, Wisconsin,' Bob introduced himself, extending his hand.

'Monsieur Brown from Milwaukee, thank you,' replied Hubert, shaking the proffered hand. 'It seems as if your country always arrives just in time to save us,' he added. 'Look at this!' and he put his bottle of wine down on a pile of *L'Illustration* magazines before going over to the shutters which had been crow-barred open. 'I was sure something like this would happen; I said so!' wailed Hubert. 'These cellars belong to Berthier, and to Madame Merlino, who suggested having the clear-out . . .'

'Bastards,' muttered Bob, who had followed Hubert.

'As you say,' agreed Hubert. 'Abby, Monsieur Chauveau, perhaps you'd better go and see whether your cellars have been broken into too.'

Magalie and Julien went down the corridor to check.

Hubert was upset by the nocturnal break-in, and also mortified by the arrival of the amiable American, who had rescued him, but who would no doubt recount the drama of his arrival to all his friends on the other side of the Atlantic. What impression of France, of Paris would that give the Americans? Even worse, what would they think of 18 Rue Edgar-Charellier? That it was a hovel pillaged by maurauding thugs who locked the inhabitants in their cellars like rabbits in their hutches.

'Our cellars are fine, Monsieur Larnaudie!' cried Julien from the corridor where the bare light bulbs cast his shadow and Magalie's on the walls.

'Well, that's something, I suppose,' muttered Hubert. 'But I bet they'll be back now they know that they can get in. Them, or others; while we're all asleep.' So saying, he raced up the wooden stairs to the street and tried to manipulate the shutters. 'It's impossible to close them,' he railed.

'Why is there an opening to the street there?' asked Bob.

'It's for coal deliveries,' said Julien; 'each cellar used to have a coal hole, and the apartments all had a fireplace in every room.'

Bob nodded, admiringly.

'I'm going to stay here,' declared Hubert.

'You're joking! You can't spend the whole night here.'

'I can and I will, Abby! Never let it be said that this building has been left unprotected in its hour of need.' Hubert sounded agitated. 'Because of my position as chairman of the management committee, and my family history, it falls to me to defend . . . our patrimony!' he concluded emphatically.

'Wait a moment, please . . .'

Bob, too, went up the steps and looked closely at the rudimentary shutter fastenings. When he came back down, he began to search through the abandoned items in the communal cellar: metal shelving, enamel worktops, hangers . . .

'What's he doing?' asked Hubert when Bob bent down and picked up a large iron rod and brandished it proudly.

'Yes! You will sleep tonight, Monsieur Larnaudie. May I?' asked Bob.

Hubert stepped down to make way for Bob, who examined the fastenings of the two shutter doors and verified that the holes they slotted into were the same diameter as the rod. 'I see what you're trying to do, but you won't be able to; you'd need to bend it for that to work,' said Hubert wearily.

'True,' said Bob, and he took off his jacket, revealing his sleeveless T-shirt and the impressive tattoos on his biceps, one of which depicted a spread eagle, its talons clutching a motorbike wheel.

Bob sat down on a step, cracked his neck, first to one side, then the other, and took hold of the rod at either end. Then he took a deep breath, clenched his jaw and began to try to bend the rod. The other three stayed very still, watching as the rod slowly began to move, unconsciously also clenching their teeth as if they were physically helping. Bob's arm muscles bulged with the effort of pushing, making the eagle's head move. Julien was surprised to find that he knew what kind of eagle it was. A client at Harry's Bar had told him. It was the bald eagle, the national emblem of the United States. Bob exhaled and drew breath. The rod now formed a perfect U-shape and he looked at it, satisfied. 'Yep, that'll do.' He went up two steps. The rod slipped perfectly into the holes.

The shutters were closed!

'Monsieur . . .' began Hubert.

'Call me Bob.'

'Bob,' Hubert corrected himself, 'I must thank you a second

time. I don't want you to think that you have spent all those hours flying here only to find yourself bending iron rods in some old dump! I would like France, that is to say Paris, and this apartment building, to welcome you in a dignified manner. Abby, Monsieur Chauveau.' He turned to Magalie and Julien.

'You can call me Julien,' Julien offered timidly.

'Very well,' continued Hubert, 'so, Abby, Julien and Bob, I'd like to invite you up to my apartment to share one of the finest products of our country – wine! I found a decent bottle in my cellar.'

Hubert went over and retrieved the bottle of wine, which he flourished triumphantly: '1954, what do you say to that? I really hope it's good.'

The colour drained from Julien's face when he saw the label.

Magalie had only been in the Larnaudies' *salon* once before, and that had been more than three years ago. She remembered a comfortable family sitting room, with exactly the kind of decor you would expect from people for whom money had never been an issue. Anyone who lived there would feel protected by something solid yet impalpable that seemed to emanate from every inch of the room. The carpet and the rug on the floor, the wallpaper, the large sofa, the Louis XVI armchairs, the paintings and the objects on the sideboard were all reassuring. As was the white marble mantelpiece characteristic of Haussmann buildings, with its bronze mantel clock reflected in the gilt mirror. Magalie was certain that if Hubert were to produce a photo of the room taken fifty or a hundred years ago from the old family album, it would be a question of spot the difference, so similar would the photo be to what was here now.

It was very unusual for Hubert to invite anyone into his home on the spur of the moment, let alone complete strangers, which they all were, apart from Abby, and he could not help thinking that Charlotte would not have been best pleased had she been there. She was always so concerned about whether he had eaten. Well, he was going to do better than that, he was going to drink. A good bottle of wine, with nice people.

Finally, some spontaneity and good luck had arrived to brighten his grey autumn days.

'Sit down, please,' he said, putting the wine on the coffee table. 'I'll be back in a moment.'

'Would you like any help?' asked Magalie.

'No, thank you, Abby. Why don't you and Julien sit on the sofa. Bob, you could take this bergère.'

Bob wasn't sure what Hubert had said. At the French Institute in Milwaukee they had studied a poem about '*un prince et une bergère*'. Surely *bergère* meant shepherdess? In the poem the shepherdess had been a girl of modest means who looked after the sheep in the meadows. Obviously, there were no sheep or shepherdesses here.

'Bergère,' said Magalie, tapping one of the arms of the chair.

Bob shrugged, indicating he still didn't understand, but he sat down anyway and looked around the sitting room. The room was like the ones he'd seen in old black-and-white French films. But in colour. It was a far cry from the way his house looked in Milwaukee. Typically French, he thought. 'Everything is very old here,' he whispered, leaning towards Magalie, who nodded.

'Here we go,' said Hubert, coming back into the room.

He put four wine glasses and a plate of crackers on the table, then picked up the corkscrew.

'I was saying that everything is very old here, very typically French,' said Bob.

And Magalie murmured to Julien with a wink, 'I've lived here since 1868 . . .'

Hubert broke off from cutting the foil covering the cork to tell Bob, 'I've lived here since 1868.'

Bob repeated the date and raised his eyebrow. Hubert gave his customary smile, and Magalie exchanged a conspiratorial look with Julien, who immediately concentrated on the bottle.

'It was my family who built this apartment building. I've lived here all my life and my father before me, and before him, my grandfather and before that, my great-grandfather. And so on back to the time of Napoleon III. I'm a true Parisian, and that's rare these days.'

Bob nodded, impressed. 'So the name in the elevator, that's yours?'

'Yes, it is. Name of Anatole, my great-great-grandfather. That's him.' He pointed to a painting of a severe-looking old man with a goatee beard and watch chain, staring out at them angrily.

'You must know everything about the history of the neighbourhood.'

'Oh, yes! For example, Abby's studio used to be a carpet shop and before that a hardware store, Ménard et Filles. I remember that closing when I was a child; it was run by Louise Ménard, who wasn't very pleasant. Before that, the shop sold silks from Lyon, and when the building was first inhabited, it was an antique shop called Au Casque d'Or. The building itself was created on the site of Saint-Martin Abbey, which burned down during the French Revolution and fell into ruin. Our building stands on the exact spot where the abbey church once stood.'

'There's a story attached to this bottle, Monsieur Larnaudie.' It was Julien, silent up until this moment, who had just spoken, quickly, almost breathlessly.

'A story? You're right, Julien,' replied Hubert, inserting

the screw into the cork. 'It must have been bought by my grandfather. Maybe he didn't have time to drink it, and then it was forgotten about for sixty years, in the chaos of the cellar.'

'No . . . I was referring to something else, Monsieur Larnaudie,' said Julien. 'Something that happened in 1954 over the Saint-Antoine vineyard.'

Hubert stopped opening the bottle and everyone looked at Julien, who ploughed on. Even though he had promised himself never to talk about flying saucers in front of any woman he was interested in, it would be impossible to drink a glass of this wine without relating what had happened to Pierre Chauveau. Was he about to lose all credibility in Magalie's eyes? After the management committee meeting she had invited him into her studio to see the broken statue. But then Bob had knocked on the window. Julien felt that an understanding had started to develop between them, which had only been strengthened by the break-in to the cellars. But now maybe it was going to evaporate. As Julien began to tell them what had happened on the night of 16 September 1954, he worried he was taking a big risk. He told them about the spaceship that had appeared above Jules Beauchamps's vines, the statement made to the police, the nickname given to his great-grandfather, the exceptional vintage produced that year, the showing of Spielberg's film. He left nothing out.

'And he disappeared with his dog?' asked Hubert.

'Yes, he was never seen again. My family still think he drowned in a pond, but he didn't say he was going boating that day, and Ausweis, the dog, could swim. She would have come back.'

There was a silence. 'What a story.' Bob was the first to speak. 'In Milwaukee, there was a man who said he saw a flying object . . . but he was a bit strange . . . so maybe that doesn't count.'

'I believe in flying saucers,' said Magalie. 'Why shouldn't there be any? There are plenty of meteorites.'

Julien turned to her. If he hadn't stopped himself, he might have gone down on one knee then and there and asked her to be his wife.

'My family also had someone disappear,' said Hubert. 'But it's not as interesting as your story. It was Cousin Léonard who vanished, Léonard Larnaudie. He lived on the third floor, overlooking the courtyard, opposite my apartment. In the 1930s he decided to go and make his fortune in Chile — he wasn't married, had no children and nothing to lose. I think he was also slightly mad. Anyway, five years later, he sent a signed postcard from Santiago simply saying, "It's done!" We never heard from him again. Had he really made a fortune? No one ever knew. He became a legend in our family, Cousin Léonard. His apartment lay empty for more than twenty-five years. The family finally sold it at the end of the 1950s, for nothing, to make up for the money lost in Suez Canal shares.'

'Shall we open it?' asked Magalie, indicating the bottle.

Hubert released the cork with a satisfying pop, and held it up to sniff it. 'Very promising. Let's taste it. I hope we're not all going to disappear,' he joked.

He poured out the wine. They all swirled their glasses and breathed in the bouquet, then Hubert raised his glass and the others followed suit.

'My friends, we are about to drink more than a wine: we're

going to drink . . . a bygone age. A liquid that's been in this bottle since 1954. This bottle was laid down in a different France, a different world. Back then, it was the Fourth Republic; the president was René Coty; people were going to see the films of Jean Gabin and were listening to Édith Piaf sing on the radio; few French people had televisions, and more than a quarter of the population still lived off the land. All that is contained in what we are about to drink . . . To a bygone age!' Hubert held his glass out and they clinked with a crystalline tinkle.

'To a bygone age! Chin chin!' said Magalie.

'To France!' said Bob.

Hubert went one better. 'To France, good wine and friendship!'

'It's excellent,' declared Magalie after the first sip.

'I'm not sure if it's because of the flying saucer but it tastes as good as a Chambolle-Musigny,' commented Hubert.

Julien agreed.

'And Julien knows what he's talking about, he's a barman at Harry's Bar,' Magalie added for Bob's benefit.

'Harry's Bar? That's very well known in America; I plan to have a drink there.'

'How about tomorrow?' Julien suggested to Bob. 'On me; it will be a pleasure.'

The wardrobe, bed, cooker, fridge, crockery, clawfoot bathtub . . . not to mention the 'Little Book of the Apartment: a guide for guests of Rue Edgar-Charellier' recommending local restaurants, grocery shops, bakeries, cafés, banks, metro lines and bus stops: Bob's host, Madame Renard, clearly thoroughly deserved the thirty-seven enthusiastic comments on her Airbnb page. The apartment was made up of a living room and adjoining bedroom, a kitchen, bathroom and small terrace with two patio chairs, a small table and a potted shrub. In the distance, Bob thought he could just make out the dome of Sacré-Cœur above the dark mass of buildings. He would have another look in daylight tomorrow. Everything was perfect and his stay in Paris had got off to the best possible start. He felt very lucky to have been welcomed into a Parisian home so soon after his arrival, and by a true Parisian to boot. He had already met three people in the building who could tell him everything he needed to know about the city. Goldie would be proud of him. He was longing for a shower, but first he began to unpack his bags. He carefully took out his HOG Milwaukee Chapter black leather vest and laid it over the back of the chair. Then he opened the white envelope he had kept with him throughout his journey. Inside were three thousand dollars in hundred-dollar bills – his spending money for the week. He would go and change them into euros first thing tomorrow.

Through the wall, Magalie could hear her new neighbour's shower running. She pulled the sheets up over her chest. Nestling under her left breast was a tattoo of a cat representing Amenophis III, a pet owned by Magalie's maternal grandmother; it was she who had raised Magalie.

Six floors down, sitting at the computer in his living room, Julien was noting down a new cocktail recipe. It was inspired by the violet scent he had smelled on Magalie's cheek earlier when, for the first time, he had kissed her goodnight.

They had drained the bottle down to the last drop, the wine had loosened their tongues and the evening had been one of the most enjoyable Hubert could remember. He had even dug out the family album and shown them photos from 1954. As Magalie had suspected, the living room was almost unchanged. The pictures showed Hubert's grandparents, his father in officer's uniform – this was the year of his military service – and the children playing with Pitch, his grandfather's basset hound who would apparently refuse to pee on walks, saving it for the doormat on his return. He was about to offer them all a glass of green Chartreuse when he and his fellow residents realised their new friend might need a rest. Out on the landing, Hubert shook Julien's hand and offered his hand to Bob. 'Hug, Hubert!' the American said, taking Hubert in his arms and slapping him on the back. Americans were so good at this stuff – if they liked someone, they wrapped their arms around them, like a child clutching a toy. It was natural and generous, a million miles away from our cold European handshakes and excessive formalities. Hubert was so carried away, he had even kissed Abby on the cheek, noticing as he did so that she smelled of violets. An American biker who rode a Harley, a neighbour who dressed like a goth and a barman from Harry's Bar – 'What unusual people! What interesting friends!' Hubert exclaimed to himself as he rinsed the wine glasses under warm water. He would never meet people like this at Sofreg.

For the past eighteen years, he had run the central Paris department of one of France's biggest property management companies. Leading a team of five, he spent his days monitoring market fluctuations, ensuring rents were paid and negotiating purchases on behalf of his clients. He had an appointment at ten the next morning with Archibald Van Der Broeck, a Belgian retail mogul with a sizeable Parisian real-estate portfolio, who met Hubert annually to go over his investments. Overweight and constantly out of breath, Van Der Broeck would host business breakfasts in his suite at Hotel Meurice rather than come to Sofreg's offices. He took the largest suite, the Dalí, which was decorated with prints of the late Surrealist genius's works and boasted a huge terrace overlooking the Tuileries Gardens. Hubert had put all the paperwork on Van Der Broeck's rental properties and ongoing transactions in his briefcase, ready for his client to sign. Might they have breakfast out on the terrace? Hubert went to the window, opened the curtains and looked at the thermometer. Nine degrees at 11 p.m. It might just be warm enough to sit outdoors the next morning. Looking down at the street below, his eye was drawn to the shop sign which read BOUVIER – CHARCUTERIE TRAITEUR – MAISON FONDÉE EN 1954. It had closed down three months ago. The windows had been boarded up and the place was being gutted. Hubert smiled ruefully. The shop dated back to the same year as the wine – soon every trace of that era would be gone for good. Word had it the lease had been taken on by a mobile-phone shop.

'*This is France Info, it's eight o'clock and you're listening to the news with Céline Dancourt. Two terrorist attacks in Istanbul last night have left at least sixty-seven dead. While no organisation has so far claimed responsibility, the Turkish authorities say the attacks bear the hallmarks of so-called Islamic State. Our correspondent, Amélie Lafarge, is in Istanbul.*'

'*At ten o'clock last night, in this busy part of the city, two devices—*'

Hubert switched stations.

'*. . . and the Heritage Days are going to last three days from today, with the RATP network marking 111 years since the first buses came into service on the streets of Paris. Owners of vintage cars who've signed up to the scheme are being encouraged to take them out on the roads and park for free, an initiative by Paris, Lyon and Marseille city councils to give everyone a chance to see these utterly unique vehicles—*'

'That's enough!' exclaimed Hubert. 'Utterly unique! They're either unique or they're not!'

Infuriated by the lax grammatical standards of radio presenters these days, Hubert flicked over to an old Dire Straits hit and then caught a snippet of a rap which seemed to display a certain hostility to the work of the police force. Hubert turned on his electric razor, drowning out the sound of the radio. He took a shower, got dressed, did up his tie, checked himself in the mirror and put on his trench coat and scarf – it might be windy on Van Der Broeck's terrace. He checked his phone for emails. The wheel span and a message came up on screen: 'Important update required'. He clicked 'Update now'.

Hubert was dazzled as he made his way out of the building. The air was much warmer than he had imagined and the sun had come out. He took off his scarf, squinting in the light. Across the road, work had resumed on the old charcuterie. Hubert walked towards the building site. Labourers were hard at work, overseen by a large moustachioed man in a flat cap.

'I'm the new owner. Do you live round here?'

'I was born here,' Hubert replied curtly, 'and I'm very sad indeed to see the previous shop close. It's been here all my life.'

'Oh, I can imagine. But that's the way of things, isn't it? Businesses come and go. You'll be very welcome in my shop.'

'Thank you, I won't be needing anything . . . You know, I remember a world in which the phrase "I'm going to take a photo with my phone" was meaningless.'

Feeling satisfied with his repartee, Hubert turned on his heel.

The other man looked blankly after him. Pushing his cap back with his thumb, he sighed, 'This isn't going to be simple.'

'Hey, boss!' shouted a voice. 'Where d'you want the chopping board? By the big counter or the little one?'

'Coming, lad!' And the man with the moustache got back to work.

As he walked, Hubert mused that the new owner did not

seem like a typical mobile-phone salesman. They were usually young, with gelled hair, and spouted words like cloud, 4G, Bluetooth, streaming, PIN code and PUK code. A horn sounded lightly. 'Yes, all right,' said Hubert. The driver gave a friendly wave and Hubert moved to make way for a Citroën Traction turning left.

A hundred yards further on, he crossed the market street and stopped abruptly at the sight of a woman with a vegetable barrow. It had been more than forty years since he had last seen women hauling carts of fruit and vegetables through the streets, sometimes asking the local kids for help in exchange for an apple or a bunch of grapes. They must have sent people out to play old-fashioned traders for the Heritage Days.

'What a wonderful sight, Madame,' Hubert called over. 'One never sees these little carts of wonderful vegetables any more. It really takes me back to my childhood.'

Wrapped in a headscarf, the woman looked back at him but said nothing.

'All these beautiful grapes,' he went on ruefully. 'If I wasn't on my way to the office, I'd take a few off your hands.'

'Why let that stop you?' cried the woman. 'Go on, take your pick! Your office ain't going to eat them. Don't have a stomach, does it?'

'No, you're quite right!' Hubert replied, a little taken aback.

The woman had really thrown herself into the part. Perhaps she was a jobbing actress hired by the local council.

'I'll come back this evening,' Hubert said.

'I won't be here this evening, Mr Tall, Dark and Handsome. You'll have to come back next week.'

'The Heritage Days will be over next week,' Hubert said with a trace of regret.

'It's a Heritage Day every day of the week with me! My heritage grows in the garden all year round!' the stallholder shouted to anyone who would listen. 'Right then, my lovely, will it be your usual carrots and a cabbage?' she said as a woman in glasses approached and gave a nod.

Hubert walked away. He couldn't remember the last time someone had called him tall, dark and handsome. At fifty-four years of age, with a sprinkling of white amid his dark-brown hair, it was really rather reassuring.

When he got to the bus stop, he had to admit that the RATP had not done things by halves. The JC Decaux bus shelter had been taken down during the night and replaced simply by an old-fashioned lamppost with the number of the bus displayed at the top. Three people were waiting. 'Even I don't remember bus stops this old,' said Hubert to the two men and young blonde woman, who smiled politely at him in response.

'Look at that! An open-platform bus, it really is like going back in time!' Hubert pointed to the vintage bus that had appeared at the end of the street.

The young woman prudently moved behind one of the men, who gave her an understanding little nod. 'Sad,' muttered the man and the girl agreed, casting a pitying look at Hubert.

'They're not dangerous.' The other man joined the conversation. 'I have a cousin like that. He finds everything amazing, whether it's a blade of grass, a car or a cloud. We found him work in the civil service; he licks stamps. It's the perfect occupation for him.'

On the platform, the bus conductor in his uniform and cap unhooked the safety rope to let the passengers on. The young woman looked indulgently at Hubert as he let her and the two men get on before him. He showed his Navigo pass to the conductor, who merely glanced at it briefly. Hubert asked, 'Are you going the usual route?'

'Of course – what do you think? That we'd be going to Deauville?'

'What would I not give to be going to Deauville,' said a young man as the bus set off noisily.

'Me too,' sighed the young woman from the bus stop.

'And me!' added the conductor, eyeing her up quite openly. 'I'd be able to see you in your bathing suit!' The young woman shrugged, pretending to be embarrassed.

'No need to go that far away, I'd be happy to take the young lady to the Deligny swimming pool.' This from an elegant-looking man. The woman beside him gave him a nudge.

'Your wife doesn't look too happy about that!' retorted the young woman.

'She's not my wife; this is my sister, my big sister, who's been keeping an eye on me since I was so high. It's true, isn't it?'

'It's good to have a sister,' the conductor said. 'It means you understand women from a young age. I'm the third in a family of six, all boys – women are a closed book to me!' Everyone on the platform smiled.

'But you have a wife, it would seem?' said the elegant man, pointing to the conductor's wedding ring.

'I do, indeed! And four daughters. There are five women in the house. I went straight from the barracks into a convent!'

There was general laughter at this. Hubert was amazed at how good-natured it all was. He couldn't remember the last time he had seen people talking to each other on the bus like this. It must be the ancient model of bus and the platform open to the fresh air that helped make for a relaxed atmosphere.

Hubert got off at his stop, removed his raincoat and stuffed his scarf into his bag. He walked up Rue de la Paix, glancing in at the Cartier window, where rivers of diamonds were lavishly displayed on blue velvet cushions. On Place Vendôme, two old-style Rolls-Royces waited outside the Ritz. A well-dressed man who bore a passing resemblance to the Duke of Windsor got out of one. Hubert realised that it wasn't only the RATP who had gone to town on the vintage vehicle theme. Obviously, many people, probably members of automobile clubs, had brought out their vintage cars for the day. A Hotchkiss and a 4 CV passed him, going towards Opéra. When he reached Hotel Meurice, he took out his phone to check the time but was greeted by 'No service'. Hubert sighed and looked instead at his watch. All the technology in the world could not replace the best mechanical watch movement, he said to himself as he drew back his sleeve. He was bang on time for his client and went in through the revolving door. It seemed to him that something was different about the lobby, but the concierge desk was still in the same place.

'I've come to see Monsieur Van Der Broeck; I'm Monsieur Larnaudie.'

The slim, grey-haired concierge obliged by opening the hotel register, a large golden leather-bound book with metal corners, and running his finger down the list of handwritten names. 'Vandermeich, Vanloo, Vanderbilt . . . Could you give me that name again, Monsieur?'

'Van Der Broeck, Archibald Van Der Broeck,' repeated Hubert.

'I'm sorry, but we don't have a guest by that name.'

'But I have a meeting arranged with him here! He sent me an email last week.'

'I beg your pardon, Monsieur?'

'You don't know Monsieur Van Der Broeck? He comes here once a year. He's well built, or . . . frankly, overweight, and he always stays in the Dalí Suite.'

'The Dalí Suite?'

Hubert smiled with the exasperated air of someone forced to waste his time explaining the obvious. 'The Dalí Suite is on the top floor and is named after the painter, Salvador Dalí, who always stayed in this hotel when he came to Paris. Perhaps you are new here?'

'I've worked here for fifteen years and I know who Salvador Dalí is,' the concierge replied tartly. 'But there's no Dalí Suite here, there's . . .'

The concierge broke off, staring at something over Hubert's shoulder, a disturbance in the lobby. From behind Hubert, a guttural voice with a strong Spanish accent rich in lingering vowels and staccato consonants shouted, 'It's cauliflower that's important!' Hubert turned to see a dark man with slicked-back hair and an upturned moustache whose tips reached to his cheekbones. He was in suit and tie and held a cane in his right hand, while in his left he brandished a cauliflower. A dozen photographers surrounded him, and a journalist, his tape recorder slung over his shoulder, held out a microphone.

'Apart from the cauliflowers, Maître, have you anyone with you?' enquired the journalist.

'I only have . . . Da-lí! But cauliflower is what matters.'

'Cauliflower?'

'Yes, cauliflower! Because it has a totally divine and paranoiac form which means . . . Monsieur is staring at me.' The man with the moustache pointed the knob of his cane at Hubert. 'It's because he knows: *Jésus, c'est du fromage!*'

He came over and his blazing eyes locked on Hubert's. In a conspiratorial tone, he repeated the words, '*Jésus, monsieur, est une montagne de fromage* . . . Yes!'

Then he span round, and pursued by his entourage of photographers, strode out of the hotel leaving Hubert standing in the empty lobby. He turned towards the concierge who smirked. Hubert then left himself, going back out through the revolving door.

On the forecourt outside the hotel, a Cadillac waited while the Spaniard continued to harangue the journalists in his staccato voice, his forefinger jabbing the air decisively, 'That is why! . . . You are all invited this evening to the Tuileries Gardens, for the throwing of cauliflower at the rhinoceros statue!'

Then he got into the back of the Cadillac, and a bellboy in a red uniform closed the door.

'Where are you going?' cried one of the journalists.

'To buy some *fromage*!' And he brandished his cane out of the open car window.

Hubert watched, transfixed, as the Cadillac disappeared towards Place de la Concorde. 'Who's that?' he asked the bellboy, tonelessly.

The boy smiled and replied proudly, 'That's Salvador Dalí!'

Hubert loosened his tie and walked rapidly back home, trying as best he could to make sense of the morning's events. Unless it was a dream, Salvador Dalí was staying at Hotel Meurice, all the buses were vintage, street sellers had reverted to using hand-drawn carts and the large moustachioed man surveying his building work whom he'd greeted as he left this morning was none other than Monsieur Bouvier himself, the founder of the charcuterie of that name. The charcuterie that had opened in 1954. Hubert stopped. 1954. The same year as the wine. He looked around him. Every single vehicle appeared to have gone back in time by more than sixty years. The road was no longer tarmac, it was paved, and no one was wearing jeans or trainers or carrying smartphones. No sign of any headphones either. All the women were in skirts, and the men in suits.

'We've gone back in time to the year of the wine,' he murmured and tottered to a bench to sit down.

The 'we' he had uttered was a beacon of hope like a glow-worm in the night: perhaps he was not alone in his plight.

'What I would like to see is General de Gaulle back in power!' declared the man drinking a Picon-bière.

Julien thought this was a perfect example of why alcohol was bad for you. Curiously, no one else seemed to find the customer's statement in any way peculiar. A workman in overalls enjoying his morning glass of white merely shrugged. Perhaps everyone felt sorry for the poor man.

Julien had dropped into this little café on his way to Harry's Bar. He had spotted a vintage bus and decided to take it to work but it left just as he reached the bus stop. He had looked up at the electronic screen to find out when the next bus would be, but the screen had disappeared, along with the bus shelter. There was an old-fashioned lamp post instead. As it was unexpectedly sunny, Julien decided that a walk would be the best way to start his day.

'Don't you agree? Isn't the leader of Free France the one we all need now?' the first man went on, looking at Julien.

'Uh, yes, yes . . .' replied Julien.

'Come on, Marcel, stop bothering the customers,' said the owner, who must have weighed getting on for twenty stone.

Marcel shook his head, reaching for his packet of Gauloises and lighting up. They certainly were tolerant here, thought Julien. You heard of some cafés who still let their customers smoke after hours, but never during opening time. Julien considered making a comment, but was a bit wary of upsetting the owner, given his size. In any case, the owner didn't seem bothered; he was busy dunking his croissant in his bowl of coffee. The smell of cigarette smoke was so unusual these days. At the other end of the bar, someone struck a match against the counter and lit their pipe. The waiter called for one large white and one small black coffee, and the owner put his croissant down to go and make them. There was a charming, antiquated feel to the café reinforced by the old advertising posters decorating the walls. One was for Dubonnet, 'Dubo, Dubon, Dubonnet', one for Byrrh and another for Berger Blanc. The old man next to Julien, who had a long beard and rings on his fingers, was reading an antiques magazine. Julien could see black-and-white photos and descriptions of various items offered for sale or exchange by collectors.

'How much do I owe you?' Julien asked. The owner had gone back to eating his croissant and as he had his mouth full, he held up three fingers. Julien looked surprised: three euros in this little place? Vintage decor obviously came at a price, or else this was how the owner paid his fines for letting customers smoke. He wanted to remonstrate, but then his eye fell on the notice pinned above the shelf of liqueurs. Written in red ink that allowed no ambiguity, the notice read: 'HERE what the proprietor says goes. The Management.' Julien placed three euro pieces on the counter and started to walk out.

'Not so fast! What am I supposed to do with this funny money?' the owner called.

'Excuse me?'

'Your coins. I'm not a collector, you know.'

'But I am,' said the old man who had been standing next to Julien. He picked up a euro and took a magnifying glass from his pocket. 'That's strange, but it's well made. It must come from a slot machine in Las Vegas. Have you been to Las Vegas?'

'Yes, I have,' mumbled Julien.

'Your coffee for these chips, young man – deal?' proposed the bearded man, scrutinising Julien. 'Done!' he cried, as Julien, whom the owner was looking at suspiciously, said nothing.

The antiques collector looked again at the coins. 'It must be a large casino, Euro; the name is marked on the chips, and 2012 is the series number. I know people who'll be interested in these.'

Outside, Julien marvelled at the bizarre café he had stumbled on, where you could smoke with impunity and people thought euros were slot-machine tokens. But he didn't have time to pursue this line of thought because a cellar window like the one Monsieur Larnaudie was obsessed by caught his eye and he stopped. The shutters were open and several very large sacks of coal were standing in front of them. A man emerged, his face sweaty and covered in black dust.

'What's all the coal for?'

The man looked up at Julien. 'What's it for?' He was out of breath. 'For fun, sonny. I lug coal down into all the cellars in the street for fun! I'm having fun here, then afterwards I'll go and have fun opposite, and then next door. And you, what do you do for fun?'

'I'm a barman.'

'Oh yeah? Well, scram and have fun in your bar, before I kick your arse.' And the man disappeared back through the cellar opening.

'What's going on here?' asked a passing policeman with a handlebar moustache.

'What's going on is that this little bugger is winding me up!' shouted the man from inside the cellar.

The policeman looked angrily at Julien.

'Making fun of a worker, you little anarchist?'

'Not at all,' stuttered Julien. 'I'm not making fun of anyone.'

'"Officer", you're supposed to address me as "Officer",' said the policeman, finger raised.

'Officer,' repeated Julien.

'Asking what my coal was for?' the other man said. 'How insulting is that?' And he grabbed a sack that must have weighed a ton.

'You show him, by God!' replied the policeman. 'Come on now, young man, time to move on. I can't have you making trouble on my patch.'

'Officer! Officer!' called a young woman, out of breath.

'What's wrong, Miss?'

'A cyclist has fallen over on my street, and he can't get up again.'

'I'm right behind you,' cried the policeman, setting off in the girl's wake.

Julien watched them go, then reluctantly moved off himself. He was startled by a sharp cry, '*Viiitrier!*' A glazier walked slowly along, panes of glass in a carrier on his back, and every few steps he gave the street cry of his trade: '*Viiitrier!*'

'*Vitrier!*' called a young woman from her balcony and the glazier looked up. 'Second door on the left.'

The glazier threw his cigarette away and pushed open the door to the building. Julien looked at his watch. Time for him to make his way to Harry's Bar so that he would be ready for service at midday.

Hubert wasn't able to enter the door code, B 34 18. That was because the keypad at 18 Rue Edgar-Charellier was no longer there. It had been replaced by a doorbell that Hubert had never seen before. That must be what they used to call the *cordon*, he thought. In days gone by, the front door to the building had been locked at night after ten o'clock. You had to press this button, which operated a bell inside the concierge's apartment. The concierge would then pull a cord above her bed that would activate the opening of the door. Once inside, visitors were expected to state their name, or the name of one of the residents. This system, which irritated everyone – the concierge as well as the residents – pertained up until 1958. Hubert stepped back to get a better look at the façade of the building. Everything else seemed exactly the same. The wooden carriage entrance, the shutters. Everything . . . except Abby's studio. DROGUERIE MÉNARD & FILLES was now written in yellow on a green background, over the shop entrance. And through the large windows could be seen all sorts of household items. There were brooms, glass bottles, scouring brushes and assorted cloths, and the space was adorned with advertising posters of smiling housewives extolling the benefits of Marseille washing powder or Nab scouring powder. Hubert looked about him. In the distance, on a bench, he

73

could make out the dark figure of a young woman with very black hair. She was sitting very still, talking in low tones and staring at the road.

'Abby!' called Hubert. She turned her head.

Hubert's heart was hammering as he hurried over to her. It was Abby and she in turn was running towards him. When she reached him, they looked at each other, out of breath, and then Magalie flung herself into Hubert's arms, letting her bag slide to the ground. 'Monsieur Larnaudie, oh Monsieur Larnaudie! I'm so happy to see you.'

'Me too, Abby, me too,' said Hubert, hugging her.

'Saucisson?' called a man's voice.

They both turned to see a large man with a moustache bearing down on them. He held a board in one hand and an enormous knife in the other. 'Marcel Bouvier, your new *charcutier-traiteur*, formerly a meat porter at Les Halles, originally from the Auvergne. Try this, it's beef from Salers cattle.'

Hubert and Magalie looked at the man and tentatively helped themselves.

'Well?' demanded Marcel Bouvier, as they chewed the saucisson.

'Very good,' admitted Hubert, in a voice that was barely audible. 'Thank you, dear Monsieur, and welcome to the neighbourhood.'

'So you're not annoyed with me for the loss of the old shop?'

Hubert shook his head.

'Splendid, Monsieur! Monsieur . . .?'

'Larnaudie,' Hubert said quietly.

'Splendid, Monsieur Larnaudie!' And he went off towards the building site that was to be his premises.

'Abby, please tell me we're about to wake up.'

They turned in unison to look at the front door of their building, which had just opened. The concierge, who was not Madame Da Silva, but a young blonde with curlers in her hair and a pink flowery blouse, threw a pail of hot water into the gutter and closed the door again.

'Bad news for our awakening,' said Abby. 'We're in 1954, 15 September to be precise.'

Hubert may have been slow to realise they had returned to the year of the wine, but not so Magalie. She had worked it out quite quickly. The door she went through every morning from the lobby of the building into her studio had been locked from the inside, even though she was certain she had not locked it the previous evening. Magalie realised she would have to enter the studio by the street as if she were a customer. But when she went out into the sunshine, she was no less blinded and surprised by the beautiful weather than Hubert. Shielding her eyes to protect them from the glare, she took a few steps towards her shop, where she saw the clutter of the hardware store. She blinked several times and stepped back on the pavement to look long and hard at the shop sign. She was frozen to the spot and incapable of thought.

The first idea that eventually came to her was that she had been adversely affected by the solvent in the glue she used in her repair work. It was reported to be dangerous although commonly used in her line of work. Some restorers had complained of dizzy spells and vision disturbance. Magalie had never before experienced any such symptoms. She remembered that last night Hubert Larnaudie had spoken of Ménard et Filles. And here the shop was, in all its glory, with its windows full and its opening hours on the door. Only LSD or magic mushrooms could have produced this kind of virtual reality from the consciousness of the drug-taker. She thought of her friend, William, a gilder from the Ateliers Gardhier, who at the end of an evening liked to regale her with his stories of taking magic mushrooms. He maintained that after one episode he had spent the night lying in his bathtub talking to the shower head, which talked back. The pair had enjoyed a philosophical discussion of a rare intensity, spanning such universal themes as death, the afterlife, the possibility of life on other planets and the existence of God. The shower head came up with precise answers to all these questions. The following morning, William had to concede that the intellectual capacities of his bathroom fittings had severely diminished, and the shower head's gifts were now limited to the provision of hot or cold water in classic or massage mode. After that he decided not to tangle with mind-altering substances again. But, in any case, Magalie had not consumed any mind-altering substances, just a truly excellent glass of wine dating back to 1954.

She pushed open the door of the shop and a little bell rang.

'Good morning,' said the man behind the counter without looking up from the newspaper he was reading. He must have been about sixty and wore a beret.

The shop smelled of mothballs and fresh coffee. Magalie looked about her. The whole space was filled with display shelves crammed with products most of which had not been available for years. Instead of her work table, covered with broken pieces of statue, there was now a stand with dozens of tins of polish of all shades, and felt slippers that fitted over your shoes so that you could polish your parquet as you walked about. An advert on the wall showed a housewife ordering her husband to put the slippers on when he got in from the office. Magalie picked up a tin of polish. It was cold, heavy, not a mirage. She turned to the wall where she had hung her restorers' diploma. It had been displaced by feather dusters underneath the slogan 'Real feathers from happy roosters!'

She went towards the back of the shop where there was a little stove and a girl heating coffee. 'Can I help you?' the girl asked with a smile.

But Magalie was incapable of answering.

'Come and read this, Louise; there's another flying saucer in the paper, at Châtenay-Malabry, this time!'

The girl gave Magalie a conspiratorial look and leaned towards her. 'My father is obsessed with these flying saucer stories,' she whispered, rolling her eyes. Then she looked at Magalie's clothes. 'I bet you work in cabaret,' she said, her eyes shining. Magalie looked down at her boots with the silver buckles, and strapless black dress with the red-eyed cat.

'I wanted to work in cabaret too, but my father wasn't keen, and nor was my mother.' The girl pulled a face. 'So I work here, but I go to theatre school in the evenings. My friend, Brigitte, she's already quite well known, and she's going to help me get a small role in her next film. Because,' the girl said to Magalie winking, 'I'm not going to be selling feather dusters for the rest of my life.'

'What's happened to the coffee, Louise? And come and

read about this flying saucer. Reported by a lawyer, this time; lawyers are respectable!'

'Coffee?' the girl offered Magalie. But Magalie shook her head.

'Maître Briard saw a cigar-shaped flying object on Thursday evening as he was returning from his chambers. Thank you, sweetie.' He took the steaming cup. 'The mysterious object hovered in the sky then vanished in an instant.'

The shop bell tinkled and a man entered and went over to the shelf of wire brushes. He selected one and came over to the till proffering a five-hundred-franc note Magalie had never seen before. It had Victor Hugo on it. The shopkeeper opened his till with a ting and handed back some old francs, then went back to his reading. 'Maître Briard is the seven hundred and fortieth witness to have come forward since January. Look, it says so there . . .'

Magalie leaned over the paper and saw a black-and-white photo of a severe-looking man holding a sketch of a cylinder. She read the date underneath the picture: Wednesday, 15 September 1954. Monsieur Ménard picked up a pair of scissors and cut the article out. 'I'm keeping a file,' he said, 'because something is going on, I know it is! Did you want anything?'

'No,' replied Magalie, 'I'm going to think it over. Thank you, Mademoiselle, Monsieur,' and she walked out.

It was like a dream. But a dream that was surreal in its precision. The cars parked on the street, the people, the shops, everything was in the same place but nothing was the same any more. A man in a grey felt hat and tortoiseshell glasses came out of number 18, a basset hound on a lead at his side. Magalie stepped back and clung on to the warm bodywork of a grey Peugeot 203. The man bent down to the animal. 'Today, *pipi* out here and not inside,' he told the dog in no uncertain terms. 'Do you understand? You have to go during your walks!'

The hound looked up at his master and they moved off together. Magalie went to sit on a bench, feeling as if the heels of her ankle boots were sinking into marshmallow. She sat down, closed her eyes and counted to ten, like she used to when she was little. Her grandmother would say to her, 'Count up to ten and when you open your eyes again, everything will be clear.' She had got as far as eight when Hubert called her name.

'Let's go and have coffee and decide what to do,' he suggested.

'We can't,' said Magalie, 'our money isn't valid.'

Hubert stared at her. '*Mon Dieu*, you're right,' he said, leaning back against an old-fashioned grey Citroën Traction. 'It is a dream, Abby, it has to be,' he said after a pause.

'It's not a dream,' Magalie insisted, and she banged the warm bonnet. 'You hear that? That is actual metal, this is really a car, it's really a Traction; everything is real, Monsieur Larnaudie.'

'Call me Hubert,' he said wearily.

'Did you go to your office this morning, Hubert?'

'Oh, if you only knew! I also bumped into Salvador Dalí and probably the Duke of Windsor. And think of this, I don't have a wife any more, or any children and I can't even cry for them . . . because they haven't even been born yet! Up there—' he pointed to his floor of the building '—is no longer where I live; it's where my grandfather lives.'

'I know, I saw him come out with his basset hound just now.'

Hubert paled as he looked at her.

'Come on!' she said, pulling him by the sleeve. 'If you're here, the others must be here too. We've all come back to the year the wine was produced. The flying saucer, the wine, it's all linked. We have to find Julien and the American, Bob. We have to go to Harry's Bar.'

As Bob climbed the steep roads of Montmartre, he decided that Paris was exactly as he had imagined. He had got up this morning and had breakfast out on the terrace, and the sun had even shone. Yes, it really was Sacré-Cœur peeking out beyond the zinc roofs in the distance. He had made himself a coffee and cooked two eggs from the box Madame Renard had left for him. Later on, he would go to the supermarket and pick up food for dinner, as well as the ingredients to make eggs Benedict the next day – as Goldie did every weekend. While he had never actually cooked eggs Benedict himself, almost thirty years of watching Goldie do it must surely help. She would beat the egg yolks over a pan of water, whisk in the butter bit by bit until the mixture thickened, stir in the lemon juice, salt, pepper and cayenne pepper, and finally pour the sauce over a warm muffin, grilled bacon and poached egg.

Bob's plan for the day was as follows: change his dollars; visit Montmartre, using the guidebook he had bought, *Hidden Montmartre: An Insider's Guide*; drink a cocktail and say hello to his neighbour Julien at Harry's Bar; walk along the Seine; take a selfie in his HOG leather vest in front of the Eiffel Tower and send it to all his contacts; and, finally, visit the Louvre and see the Mona Lisa.

When he had finished his breakfast, he took out his phone,

snapped a picture of the view from his window and sent it to Bob Junior and Jenny with the caption '*Bonjour, Paris!*' The photo whooshed off into the ether, but then the phone died. Bob checked the router and his wi-fi connection. Everything seemed in order. He had entered the password, Fox_charellier17, correctly. He put on a denim shirt and his HOG vest with a jacket which he would whip off for the selfie. He checked he had turned off the lights and the hob, and left the apartment.

When he got to the address he had found in the 'Little Book', Bob realised Madame Renard must have made a mistake. The bureau de change didn't exist. It was a café. CHEZ MARCEL — CUISINE DE L'AVEYRON — ALIGOT, TRUFFADE ET FARÇOU. He went in and asked in his best French where he might find the nearest bureau de change.

'You want to change your currency? Not round here. You'll have to go to Opéra for that,' the large bald man inside told him. 'American?' he asked without pausing for breath.

'Yes, I am.'

'So you've got dollars? I could be interested! I'll change your money for you, and we'll do it the official way. René!' he shouted to his waiter. 'Bring me the paper.'

'I don't want to be any trouble,' said Bob.

'It's no trouble, no trouble at all,' said the owner, taking the newspaper. He licked his thumb and flicked through the pages until he reached the list of exchange rates and stock market news.

'Dollars . . . here we go!' he said, laying his hand on the page. He turned the paper round and pushed it across the counter to Bob, pointing to the relevant line with his chubby finger.

Bob leaned over. 'But it's in francs!' he exclaimed.

'Well, of course it's in francs, we're in France!'

'I thought you had the euro?'

'The euro? . . . What are you all on about?' He turned to one of his customers. 'Less than an hour ago I had a kid in here trying to palm these Euro casino chips off on me. Émile took them for the price of his coffee.'

'Émile, the antique dealer?' the customer asked.

'Well, it wasn't Émile Zola, was it?'

'Have you had Brexit here too?' asked Bob.

'Brexit?' asked the bald man. 'I don't know, I don't speak Yank. So, Uncle Sam, do we have a deal?'

Feeling slightly wary, Bob only took out two hundred-dollar bills.

'Is two hundred dollars OK?'

'Perfect! I'll give you the exact exchange, to the centime. It's better than a bureau de change here. Monsieur Marcel changes your money,' he said, pointing his thumb at himself, 'and Marcel Costes is honesty itself. Straight as an arrow, me,' he added proudly.

He pulled a pencil from behind his ear, noted down a quick calculation and headed for the till.

'That's the Aveyronnais for you,' he went on, beating his chest with his fist. 'A sou's a sou – where money's concerned, there's no messing around. Count it, Monsieur!'

He placed an impressive pile of banknotes on the bar in front of Bob and counted out every one, then made up the amount to the centime with a dozen coins, carefully stashing away the dollars in the till where, Bob noticed, a small pile already lay. Monsieur Marcel poured him a glass of white wine – 'It's on me' – and told him where to buy his book of metro tickets and which line would take him to Montmartre.

The French were way behind the times – there was nothing electronic and instead of the automatic barriers found in every other city, there was a uniformed man in a cap punching little holes in the tickets passengers handed him. He must get through thousands every day. The old carriages with their bare wooden benches were not exactly the height of comfort, and Bob noticed that nobody was looking at their phone or listening to music through headphones; rather they were all either quietly reading their books or chewing their pencils while doing the crossword. Despite globalisation, the French had not lost their soul! mused Bob. They had resisted the march of modernity, happily holding on to their traditions and way of life. Men stood up for women and there were no buskers or beggars asking for help buying a meal.

When he arrived at Pigalle station, Bob came out into the square and took in the sight of the Moulin Rouge, breathing the city air in lungfuls before heading down Rue Lepic, where stallholders were shouting to crowds of passers-by across mounds of vegetables. He passed the Café des Deux Moulins, the setting for *Amélie*, which he and Goldie had seen at the French Institute in Milwaukee. That evening, they had filled in a questionnaire about the characters and locations: Which painting does the glass man keep copying? Do you think Amélie was right to play a trick on the greengrocer, Collignon? Would you keep a garden gnome like Amélie's father does? . . . to which Bob had replied: A lunch outdoors by a French painter; yes, she was right, Collignon is a jackass; I put a pumpkin in my garden for Halloween. He could not resist stepping inside the cafe, which had a tobacco counter on the right just like in the film, even though he had read online that the counter was no longer there. You should never trust what you read on the internet, thought Bob as he ordered a coffee at the bar. When the young man handed him his drink, Bob couldn't help telling him, 'I came because of *Amélie*.'

'Amélie?' he replied. 'You're out of luck, Monsieur. It's her day off, but I can leave her a message.'

Bob gave a knowing smile.

'Just tell her Bob came to see her.'

'Bob. I'll let her know,' said the young man in all seriousness.

Bob walked back up Rue Tholozé and climbed the steps in search of Rue Norvins. He wanted to see a bronze statue mentioned in the guide called *The Man Who Walked through Walls*. The statue was a homage to the pleasingly named writer Marcel Aymé, and touching its hand was supposed to bring good luck – the hand now shone like gold from being stroked by so many tourists. He found the wall where it was supposed to be, but no statue. Just above the wall, he saw a tabby cat sunning itself on the branch of a tree, its green eyes staring down at him. It seemed to be smiling. Bob waved at it and the cat closed its eyes as if in welcome. A window opened.

'Alphonse!' a blonde woman scolded the cat. 'I'm warning you, you'd better come down. I'm not going up a ladder like last time!'

The cat looked back at her, made himself comfortable, let his tail hang down and settled down for a nap.

'Damned cat . . .' sighed the woman, closing the window.

Bob retraced his steps. He returned to Place du Tertre then

wiggled his way back down the hill, only to realise he was lost. Not that he was especially concerned: no one was waiting for him, the sun was shining, and as he walked he felt a sense of lightness he had not experienced in a long time. It was a feeling that took him back to his childhood, flicking through his first Harley-Davidson catalogues in his bedroom: the sweet sensation of having your whole life ahead of you, and feeling sure that nothing truly bad can happen for many years to come.

He passed several cafés and remarked to himself that only in Paris could you find a bistro on every street corner. Folks back home didn't take their time like this – they drank from big cups of coffee while walking down the street, making calls through hands-free sets. This city seemed to have been designed to encourage you to stop for a coffee or glass of wine every thirty yards. At the fifth café he came to, Bob chose a spot on the terrace overlooking the stone steps. Two tables away, a man with grey-white hair and heavy eyes was sitting with a glass of red in front of him, smoking an unfiltered cigarette and staring into space. The waiter came over and Bob ordered a coffee. The man at the other table was still smoking, the cigarette never leaving his lips, as if it were an integral part of his being. Two young women walked past, one of them turning to look at the smoker as she went. She stopped to whisper something in her friend's ear. The smoker watched her walk back and stop in front of his table.

'I beg your pardon . . .' she said, smiling awkwardly.

'Consider yourself well and truly pardoned,' he replied.

'Are you Monsieur Prévert?'

'Yes, my dear, that's me,' he said, his cigarette moving as he spoke.

She took a flower from her buttonhole and handed it to him.

'I picked it earlier and now I'd like you to have it, to thank you.'

The poet took it gently between his fingers.

'It's I who should thank you. I shall put it in a vase, then I'll press it and keep it as a memento of our meeting.'

The girl smiled and skipped back to her friend. Prévert watched her disappear down the steps. The guy must be popular around here, thought Bob.

'Hey, Doisneau!' called the smoker. A dark haired man in his forties came over, carrying a Rolleiflex over his shoulder.

'Stay right where you are,' he said, leaning over his camera.

'Not now please; let me have a drink in peace.'

'Go on, you won't even notice me. The light's lovely. Just look ahead and don't move.'

He turned the handle and took three photos.

'There, done.'

Then he pulled up a seat and signalled to the waiter to bring him a glass of wine.

A volley of footsteps rang out behind them and Bob turned around to see what was going on. A group of breathless children came careering down the road.

'There he is!' said one of the kids, pointing at the photographer.

'Hey, Monsieur,' said the oldest, who must have been about twelve. 'Want to take our picture? We're going to roll down the hill in a trolley.'

They all stared at him, their eyes shining.

'The thing is, you took pictures of the others last week,

and we want to be in your photos too,' said the youngest, who could not have been more than seven.

'All right, kiddos, let me finish my drink and I'll be there. Where's this hill?'

'There, on the right,' said a little girl, pointing to the corner of the road.

'Off you go, then. I'll come and find you,' said the photographer.

Nudging one another, the children scurried away. The clatter of their shoes against the cobbles was still ringing in Bob's ears when a slender dark-haired man with black-rimmed glasses took the third chair at the neighbouring table without saying a word.

The photographer was talking about the shots he had taken of butchers at Les Halles for a book he was working on. The smoker was playing with his flower.

'Everything all right? Are we boring you, Marcel?' the smoker asked.

The third member of the party had not spoken since he sat down.

'No, why? I'm very much enjoying myself,' he said.

'Right, I'm off to find those kids,' said the photographer, setting down a few coins.

'I might do some writing,' said the smoker. 'You?'

Marcel paused. 'I might do some sleeping,' he said. 'Or not,' he added.

They all stood up, shook hands and went off in different directions.

These little streets, people like 'Monsieur Prévert', the cafés and simple local life . . . Bob thought of Goldie and the empty chair facing him at the round bistro table. They could be happy living in a place like this. They had waited so long to come to Paris; perhaps it wasn't meant to be a simple holiday destination, but somewhere to settle. Maybe all roads had led to Paris since the beginning, and now that they had reached retirement and the children had grown up, it was time to take the plunge and move here. Bob opened his palm and stared at the broken lifeline the significance of which he still could not understand.

As soon as he saw them coming through the door of Harry's Bar, Julien rushed out from behind the bar and hugged Magalie tightly, momentarily grateful that the magic spell which had sent him so far back in time had also let him take her in his arms. Her scent, reminiscent of violets, and the mere touch of her body steeled him for whatever might be thrown at him, from whatever era. Then he embraced Hubert too – to somewhat lesser effect. The large, stylish man smoking a cigar on a bar stool mused that his new recruit, whose friends were already visiting within hours of him being taken on, might well be permanent staff material.

'I'll spare you the details of the whole mix-up,' Julien told the others. 'He thinks I saw the advert he placed to stand in for a sick bartender,' he said, nodding at the cigar smoker. 'He made me mix five cocktails to see if I knew my stuff, then he took me on for the day. And who is this guy but Harry MacElhone.'

When Hubert and Magalie failed to react, he went on.

'It's Harry – *the* Harry! The founder of Harry's Bar . . . who died in 1958,' he added under his breath.

Magalie nodded. 'Of course he's here, Julien. We're in 1954.'

'We've gone back to the year of the wine,' added Hubert.

'I know,' murmured Julien. 'I don't know how, but I know why. Can I get you a drink?'

'We haven't got any money,' complained Hubert.

'It's on me,' said Julien. 'I'll take it out of my pay. Let's start with a couple of Bloody Marys.'

'Three Gin Fizz, one Pimm's, three Bloody!' called out one of the barmen.

'Coming up!' said Julien, opening a shaker and reaching for a bottle.

Magalie followed each of Julien's movements: the way he tipped the bottle towards the shaker and poured the exact amount, stopping the flow with his thumb. Vodka, gin, lemonade, lemon juice, tomato juice and little bottles of Worcestershire and Tabasco sauce passed through his hands like playing cards in a magic trick. Magalie noticed that Julien had pianist's hands – she could imagine his fingers playing Bach on the keyboard of a Steinway. There were no superfluous gestures. At work in her studio, surrounded by little bottles of glue and solvents, her own movements were equally precise. Both she and Julien used their hands to unite disparate elements into one cohesive whole, bringing a smile to their customers' faces at seeing a cherished object restored, or tasting the first mouthful of a fresh and delicately balanced cocktail. What set them apart was speed: Magalie's hands needed to move slowly, Julien's at pace, but despite their differences it seemed that these two pairs of hands could perhaps understand one another.

Julien set two Bloody Marys in front of them and continued mixing the other drinks.

'*Bonjour, les amis!*'

Everyone turned to see Bob entering the bar.

'You're all here!' he exclaimed. 'Hubert, Magalie, Julien . . .'

'American?' shouted Harry from the other end of the bar.

'I'll go say hi,' Bob told the others as he headed over to shake Harry's hand.

'Bob Brown from Milwaukee.'

'Harry from Paris. Welcome home, Bob!'

'He hasn't realised,' muttered Hubert, without taking his eyes off Bob.

'Are you kidding?' said Magalie.

'How would he?' Hubert went on. 'He's never been to Paris.'

Bob came back to join Hubert and Magalie.

'Is that a Bloody Mary?' he asked, pointing at their drinks.

'Indeed it is,' Hubert replied, staring sadly into his glass, which was already less than three-quarters full.

'Julien!' called Bob. 'I'll take a Bloody Mary too.'

Julien glanced at Magalie.

'Do you like Paris?' she asked Bob.

'Yes, very much,' he said, pulling up a barstool. 'I visited Montmartre this morning. It was just like I imagined.'

'He probably bumped into Doisneau and Marcel Aymé while he was there . . .' sighed Hubert, draining the rest of his Bloody Mary.

'Bob,' Magalie cut in. 'We have something to tell you.'

After hearing Magalie's account, Bob stared back at her. He turned to Hubert, who said phlegmatically, 'I couldn't have summed it up better myself.'

'It's not possible, guys.'

'No, but it happened,' Magalie insisted. 'Look at the news-paper.' She picked up the *New York Herald Tribune* and showed him the date.

'It's just a collectors' edition,' Bob objected, after scanning the front page.

'No, it's today's paper, just like this copy of *Le Figaro*.' She held up a newspaper bearing the same date: 15 September 1954.

Julien placed another round of Bloody Marys in front of them and Hubert immediately downed a good quarter of his. Bob took a sip from his glass.

'It's very good,' he said. 'Is it true this is where the Bloody Mary was invented?'

'Yes,' replied Julien. 'And the French 75, the Sidecar and the Blue Lagoon – but that one doesn't exist yet. It'll be invented six years from now, in 1960,' he said with a strained smile, returning to his cocktail shakers.

Bob watched him go and then turned to Hubert and Magalie.

'Are you fooling with me, guys? Madame Renard—'

'Madame Renard,' Hubert cut in, gently shaking his head, 'hasn't been born yet . . . and your apartment doesn't exist, Bob. It's where the maids live.'

'But what about yours, Hubert? We were there just last night.'

'It's not mine any more,' he replied. 'It belongs to my grandfather, André Larnaudie.'

'And Magalie?'

She shook her head. 'I don't exist yet either. I won't be born until 1983. Look,' she told him, 'this bar is more than a hundred years old. The man whose hand you shook is the founder. There are portraits and caricatures of him all over the walls. How could he still be alive today?'

Bob silently scanned the room. Then he stood up, took a swig of his Bloody Mary and placed the glass back down on the bar.

'OK, let's figure this out right away. I'll ask him who's President of the United States.'

They watched Bob exchange a few words with Harry, who gave him a friendly slap on the back, smiling broadly with his cigar between his teeth. Bob came back towards them.

'Dwight D. Eisenhower,' he said after a pause. 'He also said I must be really drunk to have forgotten. Either the guy's crazy, or it's really true.'

'Option two,' Hubert said calmly, stirring his Bloody Mary.

Sitting in a row on their bar stools, they all remained deep in thought until Bob broke the silence.

'OK . . . There are problems worse than this.'

'You think?' said Hubert.

'Yes, dying is worse. No one died, we're all OK. We've got money.'

'No, we haven't,' replied Hubert.

'Yes, look,' said Bob, taking from his jacket an impressive bundle of old francs.

'How did you get those?' asked Hubert, dumbfounded.

'My dollars! I changed them all at the Opéra bureau de change. Three thousand should be enough, right?'

Hubert slowly nodded his head.

'In 1954, yes, that's a lot of money, Bob.'

'We'll share it between us.'

'We can't do that!' said Magalie.

'I insist,' said Bob. 'All four of us have a big problem on our hands, so we need to stick together and find a way out of this, starting by sharing what we've got.'

'I can't possibly accept,' said Hubert.

'Come on! You've got to. How about Lafayette?' Bob exclaimed. 'Didn't the Americans take Lafayette's cash during the War of Independence?'

'Yes . . .' Hubert conceded.

'Well, consider me your Lafayette,' Bob said resolutely.

He counted the notes into four equal piles, pushing one each towards Hubert and Magalie, tucking the third into his jacket pocket and keeping one aside for Julien, who was coming back towards them. Leaning in and looking around to check nobody was listening, Julien whispered a name conspiratorially: Charles Arpajon.

'Professor Charles Arpajon,' he went on, 'self-published his book *Alien Visits and Space Phenomena* in 1955. It's a cult classic and practically impossible to get hold of – copies go for over a thousand euros on eBay. The book tells of the events of 1954, the Year of Flying Saucers, and puts forward a theory.'

They all watched him expectantly.

'Arpajon's theory is this: UFOs don't travel through space, but through time. There are no habitable planets for galaxies around – if a spaceship wanted to come here, even if it moved at the speed of light, it would take at least a century to reach our atmosphere. So . . . if they can get here, that means they've harnessed . . . the corridors of time.'

'Three Bloody, one Singapore Sling, two Sidecars!'

'And Professor Arpajon,' Julien went on, 'is in the phone

book; I've checked. I finish my shift at six. I'll call him and arrange to see him. He'll help us – he has to,' he said confidently, surprised to hear himself sounding so authoritative.

'Is there a directory and a telephone here?' asked Hubert.

'Yes, in the basement,' Julien told him, pointing the way.

Hubert stood up, steadying himself against the bar – it wasn't every day he had two Bloody Marys for lunch.

'Living in the same place since 1868 has to be worth something!' he said firmly, heading off towards the stairs.

Bob slipped the bundle of old francs into Julien's apron pocket with a wink.

'I'll explain,' said Magalie.

A few minutes later, after splashing his face with water, Hubert came back upstairs and planted himself in front of the others.

'Done,' he said. 'At least we know where we're sleeping tonight.'

'Bernadette! Guess who just telephoned?' André Larnaudie called as he replaced the receiver.

Not getting an answer, he went to look in the library. A stern-looking woman, her hair in a chignon, sat at a grand piano, concentrating on playing. André Larnaudie could not help frowning sorrowfully at the slapdash way Beethoven's masterpiece was being rendered. 'Guess who just rang?' he repeated, and his wife jumped.

'Dear heart! I didn't see you there!' she exclaimed, her hand on her chest.

'It was Cousin Léonard!' announced André Larnaudie proudly, tucking his fingers inside his waistcoat.

'Your cousin from Chile?'

'The very same, my dear, the mythical Léonard, the millionaire!' His eyes gleamed greedily. 'He's going to be passing through Paris and he wants the keys to his apartment.'

'What does he want them for? Why now?'

'Why the devil shouldn't he have them? He may have been gone for twenty-four years, but the apartment's still his.'

'He doesn't pay any service charge, may I remind you,' said his wife, tight-lipped.

André shrugged, took out his tobacco pouch and filled his

pipe. 'You don't ask millionaires to pay a share of the service charge,' he said as he struck a match.

'Oh, don't you? What do you ask them then?'

'You ask them for stock-market tips!' said André irritably. 'Do you think I'm going to make him pay the few thousand francs he owes the building as if I were some kind of loan shark? Some little chancer? . . . I'm a Larnaudie and I'm going to talk to him as an equal.' He threw his shoulders back and walked over to the window. He took a first puff of his pipe, releasing a cloud of smoke. 'Although I would like to know how that loafer has been able to amass a fortune on the other side of the world, while we have been mouldering here.'

'Thank you for that description of us,' his wife remarked tartly.

André Larnaudie turned to his wife and looked at her without saying anything. She went back to playing the piano and he grimaced. 'Bernadette, stop that. I know Beethoven was deaf, but all the same . . .'

'What's that supposed to mean?'

'Nothing,' said André hastily. 'Séraphine!' he shouted.

His call was answered by a redhead of about fifty in an apron. 'We'll be six for dinner and I'd like duck à l'orange,' André announced.

The cook was horrified. 'It's a bit late to be telling me this now, Monsieur!'

'I'm sure you'll manage if Louisette and Marie help out. Don't make a fuss,' André said in an attempt to impose his authority.

'I'll walk out!' threatened the cook. 'Where does Monsieur think I'll find a duck now? In the pond in Parc Monceau?'

'Séraphine is right. You're being completely unreasonable,' said Bernadette Larnaudie, delighted to have this unexpected chance to put her husband in his place.

André sighed, frowning in exasperation. 'Well, what do you suggest?'

'You'll have to wait and see,' retorted the cook, turning to leave.

'Send me Marie and Louisette!' André called after her. Then, in an effort to regain the upper hand, he said, 'Well, that's that. I don't know what we'll be eating, but she has never let us down yet.'

Two girls sidled into the library.

'We're going into the apartment opposite,' André told them, 'and you two girls are going to dust and polish all the furniture.'

'The apartment opposite? The one that's all closed up?' asked Louise.

And Marie added, 'Everyone says it's haunted.'

'Utter nonsense,' said André. 'Don't be so silly!'

Pitch, the basset hound, came in and stationed himself on the carpet. He looked at the women one by one, then raised his nose towards his master, and stared at him.

'No . . .' André murmured, 'not on the carpet . . .' and he closed his eyes as the sound of a gentle waterfall could be heard.

The two servant girls knew what to do in this situation and needed no instruction. They went off to fetch the mop and soapy water.

'Why does he do that?' groaned André.

'Because he wants to hear Beethoven!' said his wife, starting to play the Moonlight Sonata again.

In the apartment opposite, Marie and Louisette opened the shutters that had been closed for twenty-four years. They swept and mopped, polished the furniture, cleaned the windows with whiting, and then returned. They came in by the service entrance opening into the kitchen, looked at each other and fled to the *salon*. 'Monsieur!' This was Louisette.

'What now? Can't you wait for me to call you?' André lowered his paper to look at the girls.

'Madame Séraphine has gone!'

The master of the house paled, put down his paper and rose to follow them to the kitchen. The lights were out and the cook's apron was folded on the worktop. She had left a carefully written note on the pad used for shopping lists:

I regret to inform Monsieur and Madame that I am leaving forthwith without my wages.

I'm taking back my liberty.

Best wishes to my successor!

Séraphine Bourellier

André Larnaudie sat down heavily on a stool and took off his tortoiseshell glasses. 'Do you know any cooks?' he said after a silence.

'No, Monsieur,' they chorused.

'Men of my station all marry women who know how to cook. Except me. All my wife knows how to do is massacre Beethoven on the piano! What a disgrace. If grandfather Anatole were to see me now! And Madame has gone off to her hairdresser. What are we going to do?'

'We could go to the *traiteur*,' proposed Marie.

'Marellier? He charges an arm and a leg for duck; that's out of the question.'

'There's also Monsieur Bouvier,' suggested Louisette, 'the new charcuterie that's about to open next door. He's offering slices of saucisson to everyone living in the neighbourhood. We could buy some from him and make up some platters, a sort of light supper. Apparently in Hollywood they're more fashionable than full dinners. I read that in *Cinémonde*.'

André Larnaudie looked at her, aghast.

It was a silly idea. Magalie knew that, but she had not been able to stop herself and now here she was standing in front of the entrance to Passage Choiseul with its two hundred yards of covered galleries. Only ten minutes on foot from Harry's Bar, it had just been too tempting. At the same time, the thought of delving into her own past made her head spin, as if she were living a dream. She would walk down the arcade and find the haberdashery, Mercerie Mercier. And then walk through the door and see Odette Mercier, the grandmother who had raised her after the death of her parents. Odette, who would be thirty-one, two years younger than Magalie.

'I can't . . .' murmured Magalie, and she retraced her steps and sat down on a bench.

Memories resurfaced like sediment stirred up by a ground-swell. Images and sounds assailed her like wind battering the doors and windows of an old empty house on the night of a storm. 'Come, my darling,' her grandmother had said, hugging her close. 'She can leave,' the doctor said. 'It's a miracle she wasn't hurt.' In the hospital room, seven-year-old Magalie had gathered her belongings into a bag, put on a duffel coat and taken Odette's hand. Together they had walked down the long corridors, passing people in white coats and others on trolleys pushed in silence by nurses. The corridors led to a bank of lifts. Odette had not been able to say a word since, 'Come, my darling,' but that was fine because Magalie Lecœur, daughter of Isabelle Mercier and Marc Lecœur, was not able to speak either. She just stared at the lift button until finally it lit up with a ping and the arrow indicated it was going down.

Sunday, 11 November 1990. Winter. The weather was beautiful and very cold. It should have been a sunny and special weekend. All three of them had set off in the car to look at houses in Sologne where Magalie's father had spent part of his childhood and where he had always hoped to buy a second home. He and Isabelle had spotted two estate-agent adverts for houses that they would be able to afford. They were both medium-sized with large gardens. And so the idea of having a weekend with their daughter out of Paris had taken shape. They would stay in a hotel in Romorantin, and as well as looking at the houses they would visit the chateaux of Chambord and Cheverny. The first house turned out not to live up to expectations, but the disappointment was mitigated by their trip to the magnificent Château de Chambord. The sight of Francis I's estate rising out of the mist that had settled on the frozen ground would remain for Magalie the last happy image of her life before tragedy struck. At 3.38 p.m., after their guided tour of the historic house and a quick lunch, Marc Lecœur's Renault 21 was speeding towards the second house viewing, when a lorry coming in the opposite direction began to flash its headlights wildly then veered into the Renault. The universe exploded. The noise was so shocking there was no noise. The collision was so violent there was no violence. There was nothing any more. The bodywork crumpled as easily as tin foil; the windows were pulverised into a million tiny pieces. The lorry slid on its side for a hundred yards and the car flipped over six times. By the fourth turn, Isabelle and Marc Lecœur were already dead, their necks broken. When firemen prised the car open with an electric saw they found a little girl, unconscious but not visibly injured. She was in a coma for six days before opening her green eyes. The police report confirmed that the lorry driver's brakes had failed and no charges were brought against him. After a long legal process, his employer paid out damages for negligence in maintaining his vehicles. The apartment was sold. Of Magalie's life before the accident, all that remained were a few photographs. Magalie went to live with her grandmother who became the centre of her world up until she too died.

'I dress like a goth, because I am in eternal mourning.'

'I dress like this because when we visited Chambord, the guide said, "The upper parts of the chateau, notably the turrets and chimneys, were built in the gothic style."'

'I repair objects broken into millions of pieces because one day my life was shattered into a million pieces.'

Thirteen years later, she was to say these three things to her psychiatrist, who was nearing retirement. He took off his glasses and let a silence fall, before replying, 'You're ready now, Magalie. Our journey together ends here. There will be no more sessions. I have rarely said such a thing before, but I'm going to say it now, probably for the last time in my career: Magalie, your analysis is complete.'

There was an optician, a coal merchant, a collectors' shop (STAMPS AND COINS FROM ALL OVER THE WORLD) and a china shop. In the next window was a full-scale automated model of a woman knitting, with balls of wool stacked up behind her. Then a locksmith, an upholsterer, and a costume-hire shop (MAKE-BELIEVE FOR ONE NIGHT: WEDDING AND COCKTAIL DRESSES, DINNER JACKETS AND BALLGOWNS). After that a florist, a framer, and a toy shop named Au Pélican, offering toy soldiers and electric trains.

Finally, Mercerie Mercier (THREADS AND RIBBONS. EVERYTHING FOR THE FINEST DRESS-MAKING).

Magalie opened the door and a bell rang in welcome. The shop was very light and the entire wall behind the counter was covered with little drawers that rose up to the ceiling, with a sliding ladder for access. Each drawer was labelled with a handwritten sticker. They contained thousands of pearl and brass buttons in all shapes and sizes. Enough to sew on to all the school uniforms of all the girls across France. When she was little, Magalie had been allowed to play at Odette's house with a box of buttons from the haberdashery. Perhaps those same buttons were already here in the shop, thought Magalie. On the left-hand wall were spools of ribbon in all colours and materials – cotton, silk, velvet, linen . . . And on the large tables were displays of lace and needle-cases in a pyramid. Magalie looked towards the staircase at the back of the haberdashery. A young woman was coming down. 'Hello,' she called cheerfully, and Magalie thought she might faint.

It was Odette! A thirty-one-year-old Odette she had never known, but whose green eyes, so like her own, she immediately recognised.

'How may I help you?' Odette asked her with a smile.

Come back! Magalie almost replied. In spite of herself, she was trying not to look at Odette directly. 'I'd like . . . some thread,' she managed eventually, looking at the cotton reels.

'There's certainly plenty of that here,' said Odette, 'enough to truss up the Eiffel Tower like a leg of lamb!'

And Magalie closed her eyes, hearing the familiar phrase, 'If only you'd known the shop, darling, we had so much thread we could have trussed up the Eiffel Tower like a leg of lamb!' As a child the image of the Eiffel Tower wrapped in thread had invaded Magalie's dreams. She took a deep breath and opened her eyes on a fine, golden thread wound round a wooden reel. She pointed at it.

'Is it for embroidery?' asked Odette.

'Yes, it's for an overcoat,' Magalie almost whispered.

'The buttonholes, I assume,' said Odette with another smile.

'Yes,' said Magalie, 'but I'd like to add some decorative stitches as well.'

'That will be pretty,' said Odette. 'In that case I would advise a fifteen needle. What sort of decoration did you have in mind?'

'Bees, on the front,' said Magalie.

'Oh yes, good idea. I sew bees as well, in satin stitch.'

'Also known as damask stitch,' replied Magalie. 'I'm going to do these in crossed satin stitch.'

'What a good idea,' Odette replied, going back to the counter to wrap the pretty reel of thread in tissue paper. 'And who taught you to do that? There aren't many young girls who know how to do crossed satin stitch these days.'

'You – it was you who taught me,' murmured Magalie, turning towards the window.

'Amenophis!' cried Odette, and Magalie turned back to see that a beautiful Siamese cat had jumped up on the counter.

'He's not a bad cat,' said Odette, 'but he can be mischievous. I have to keep him away from the ribbons.'

Magalie went up to the cat who watched her closely. 'Amenophis,' she murmured, stroking him, as he pressed against her hand.

She knew his grandson. Amenophis III had been her child-hood cat, a grey stray mixed with Siamese who had the same soulful eyes. The cat she had tattooed nestling under her left breast.

'Usually Parisian cats are called Kitty, Pussy or Titi, but I called him Amenophis because—'

'Cats come from Egypt, where in ancient times they were gods and people worshipped the cat goddess Bastet,' Magalie finished for her.

'Oh, you know that too?' said Odette. 'You know so much about sewing, and cats, we could become friends!' she joked.

Magalie looked directly at her and nodded. 'We will,' she said as the doorbell tinkled and three women entered, chattering about sewing and cross-stitch.

Magalie paid for the reel of thread and picked up the little package.

'I'll be right with you, ladies,' said Odette, accompanying Magalie to the door. 'Come back and see me again,' she said, smiling.

'I am coming back,' said Magalie quickly, turning away. Odette softly closed the door and Magalie said to herself, 'I'm coming back in thirty years,' and the shopping arcade blurred in front of her as she walked out.

'Don't cry, beautiful,' said a workman in overalls as she passed. Magalie smiled and wiped her eyes before crossing the road to the café at the entrance of Passage Choiseul.

She sat down on a banquette and ordered rum, which surprised the waiter. He made no comment, however, and went off to the bar. Magalie took her reel of gold thread from the tissue paper and rolled it between her fingers, smiling. She suddenly noticed that there was a table of young men in their twenties opposite her. Now that she was revived by the rum, her first mouthful having delivered what Odette would have called a 'shot in the arm', she could hear their animated conversation. There were about ten of them talking about film, and all smoking cigarettes, apart from the plump one with straight hair and glasses who had a pipe. The leader of the group seemed to be the very slim, fervent-looking young man with close-cropped dark hair, who spoke the most. He kept saying things like, 'It's time for action.' 'We can't go on like this.' 'The days of filming inside studios are over. We need to get outside, because that's where the stories are, and where life is.' As Magalie watched, their eyes met.

'You can make a story out of anything. If you were to film this young lady—' indicating Magalie '—you would have a story! I assure you,' he continued with a smile, 'that everything is a story and you are one too!'

'François is right,' said the pipe smoker and one of the others backed him up:

'I agree with Claude.'

François smiled at Magalie. 'What do you think, Jean-Luc?' François turned to his neighbour.

'Yes,' said a boy with tinted glasses, who had a strange sybillant delivery. 'A girl in a café and her reflection in a mirror, that's already a story . . . or two stories.'

Magalie finished her rum and left some change on the table. Then she got up and left the café, under the gaze of François Truffaut.

Peeking through the macramé curtain, the concierge, Madame Martin, watched a dark-haired man checking himself in the hallway mirror. Hubert looked at himself and took a deep breath. He was about to come face to face with his grandfather, a man he had never met and had seen only in the family album. He tried to remember the few amateur performances he had taken part in as a student at Sciences Po. His biggest roles had been as Thomas Diafoirus in Molière's *Le Malade imaginaire* and Gontran in *Monsieur chasse!* by Georges Feydeau. Way back then, he had been given time to rehearse and his lines had been supplied by two great geniuses of theatre. This time, he had no costume to hide behind, no safety net to fall back on.

Meanwhile, up on the third floor, André Larnaudie was flicking through the red velvet-bound family album in search of a photo of Léonard. After all these years, he could no longer clearly picture his cousin and one-time neighbour's face. He knew he had the typical Larnaudie dark hair, but beyond that remembered little of the jobless bachelor who had given up his law degree and spent five years living in the apartment he had inherited from his parents, keeping such a low profile that a month could easily go by without passing him in the hall. He had been twenty-nine when he left in 1930 and would be fifty-three now. He had escaped all of France's recent troubles: the weak governments of the Third Republic, the Stavisky Affair, the far-right riots of 1934, the Popular Front of 1936, the War, the Occupation, Vichy, the black market and hunger, followed by the Liberation, the purge, rationing, the departure of General de Gaulle, the Fourth Republic . . . the list of ups and downs his cousin had avoided by leaving for Chile was long. He had no doubt lived an adventurous life and picked up quite a tan while he was at it. Would the man whom André was about to meet turn out to be a veritable South American, with no trace of Larnaudie left?

As these thoughts turned in his head, André Larnaudie finally came to a picture of a ten-year-old Léonard wearing a suit and armband for his Communion. The doorbell rang. He slid the album back onto the shelf, headed out into the hall and flung open the door to Hubert.

'My dear cousin!' he cried with forced bonhomie. 'I was expecting a conquistador, but you haven't changed a bit.'

'Nor have you!' Hubert replied quickly, stepping inside the apartment.

'Oh, but I have,' André said wearily. 'I've got old. Listen, if you'd come yesterday, you would have found me in bed with a bad back – I haven't been to the office all week. Anyway, enough of that. Bernadette's so sorry to miss you, she's at the hairdresser – we didn't know you were coming, of course – but she'll be here for dinner later. Oh God, dinner . . .' he sighed. 'My cook has died.'

'Died?' asked Hubert, horrified.

'Yes, this morning, the poor woman. She was a real gem, goodness itself. I asked her to prepare a duck à l'orange for you and she was so thrilled,' he said, leading Hubert into the living room. 'She was brilliant at that dish. She really put her heart and soul into it.'

It was strange for Hubert seeing his own living room and he began to feel oddly at home again: the dresser, the bronze clock, the portrait of Anatole and the bergère chair – just about everything was here, in the same place.

'So I'm afraid we have nothing to eat but plates of Auvergne charcuterie,' sighed André.

'But that sounds perfect. How often do you think I get to eat Auvergne-style in Chile?'

'Not very,' André conceded. 'Well, if you'll forgive me the meagre dinner offering, I promise to make it up to you with the wine. I'm a bit of a buff, you see. I've a few bottles in the cellar and I'm looking forward to hearing what you and your friends think.'

Hubert let out a shudder. This quiet man would soon acquire a wine yet to be harvested: Château Saint-Antoine 1954.

Pitch entered the room and sniffed warily at Hubert, who stroked him.

'Ah, here you are, the famous basset hound. Still doing your business on the doormat?' joked Hubert, who was beginning to feel more at ease in Cousin Léonard's skin.

'How did you know?' André asked flatly. 'I didn't have this dog when you left.'

Hubert looked up at his grandfather and paused.

'Why . . . because my dog is the same!' he said, thinking on his feet. 'He holds it in when we're out and then relieves himself on the rugs in my hacienda.'

'Oh, my dear cousin!' exclaimed André, clutching Hubert's hands. 'We have one and the same problem! I can't tell you how happy that makes me. I thought I was the only one saddled with such a specimen.'

Settling down on the sofa, eyes shining, his grandfather said, 'Tell me a bit about this hacienda of yours.'

With Léonard's keys in his pocket at last, Hubert left with his head spinning. He had been forced to describe in detail his hacienda and three swimming pools, one of which was fed by a natural hot spring – did they even have hot springs in Chile? It didn't really matter – his fifteen domestic servants, three cooks and eight gardeners. His vast terrace overlooking the Monastorio valley where the sun set every evening in a blaze of colour. He had drawn the Hispanic name Monastorio from his childhood; back in 1974, he would never miss an episode of *Zorro*, shown in black and white, in which the hero's mortal enemy was Capitan Monastorio. Was there a lady to oversee this sprawling estate? Hubert spoke of his dear wife Doña Carlotta and their two children, Camilla and Oliverio, who worked alongside him, but was yet to mention anything about his vast fortune. With his friends, Bob Brown, an American businessman, Abby, his PA, and Julien, her husband, a Frenchman living in Chile who did odd jobs and even acted as his bodyguard, he had – of course – checked in to the Ritz.

'Of course,' stammered André Larnaudie.

'But, you know how it is, cousin. I'm so fed up of five-star hotels and luxuries . . .' he complained, before continuing in solemn tones: 'That's why I was so keen to come back here, where all my dreams began.'

'Welcome home, cousin!' beamed André.

Hubert could not remember using so much brainpower in such a short space of time since his viva at Sciences Po. That exam had earned him his degree, but the test he had just sat meant even more to him: he hadn't blundered, faltered or waffled, but had managed to speak convincingly about a life he had never lived, in a country whose borders he could barely trace on a map. He had even got away with the slip-up about the dog.

Hubert turned the key and entered the apartment. In the hallway he was greeted by a Greek alabaster torso mounted on a column and a series of six prints of Roman wrestlers hanging alongside a large mirror. Measuring a good thousand square feet, the apartment smelled freshly polished and remained fully furnished. In pride of place in the living room above a Chesterfield sofa was a large Art Deco painting of young men in swimwear standing beside a lake with their arms around each other's waists, seeming hesitant to enter the water. On the mantelpiece was a bronze clock like the one his grandfather owned, though, rather than Diana the huntress, it depicted a Greek shepherd gazing into the distance. The coffee table dated from the early 1920s and Hubert thought the varnished rosewood veneer cupboard beneath the tabletop might be a cigar humidor. He opened the door to find one last Havana and a cigar cutter which seemed to have been left there just for him. Montecristo no. 1. Despite twenty -four years having passed, the box had protected the cigar, the product of an island now, in 1954, ruled by Batista. Hubert held it up to his ear and rolled it between his thumb and index finger: no suspect crackling. He picked up the cigar cutter and the table-top lighter, sliced the cigar with the steel ring and lit it. He hadn't smoked a Havana cigar in almost ten years, but he felt he deserved this one, and besides, it could only help to focus his mind. He went from room to room, checking that the apartment was big enough to sleep four. Hubert noticed that every room still had its original fireplace. In the dining room he found a large green glazed earthenware stove.

'It's all still here, intact. How wonderful,' Hubert murmured, smiling to himself.

He had always regretted that this apartment no longer belonged to him. He could have knocked it through into his own or rented it out for several thousand euros a month. In 2017, this apartment belonged to the Ménard family and all the fireplaces were gone. Monsieur Ménard complained that the chimneys didn't draw properly, despite having been swept, and had blocked up the remaining two, much to the disapproval of Hubert, who had told the management committee that the removal of the fireplaces was an affront to the heritage of a period Haussmann-era property and that Monsieur Ménard should simply learn how to light a fire.

As the Havana burned down, Hubert returned to the living room to look for an ashtray but found none. He was about to flick his ash into the fireplace when he noticed a black leather-bound book sitting on the andirons. He knelt down and turned it over. The back cover was burnt and some of the edges were scorched, but it was otherwise undamaged. Balls of paper and a burnt match still lay in the grate. So Ménard was right: the apartment's chimneys really didn't draw properly. Hubert opened the cover: the words 'Diary of Léonard Larnaudie' were inscribed on the first page in beautiful fountain-pen calligraphy. He sat on the sofa and began to read.

Wednesday, 25 November 1930

I have had more than enough of this family of snakes and the 'family property', 18 Rue Edgar-Charellier. The atmosphere has become yet more unpleasant since that poisonous toad Anatole kicked the bucket at the grand old age of ninety-eight. Cousin André is leaving the fourth-floor apartment to move into Anatole's larger place on the third floor. He intends to rent his old apartment to Aunt Marguerite, pretending that it doesn't have a cellar in order to keep both for himself. I'm sick of the lot of them . . . sick of their dirty tricks. I may have been born into the bourgeoisie, but I can't stand them any longer!

I went to the Cavalier Bleu with Armand tonight. Cocteau was there at a table with friends. I went over to tell him how much I loved *The Blood of a Poet* last year. Cocteau is a lovely man, slight, with long hands, hypnotic eyes and a high-pitched voice. 'Don't tell me you're another aspiring actor?' he said. 'Not in the least,' replied Armand. 'We want to be hairdressers,' and Cocteau laughed and said he was glad to hear it. But am I really going to be a hairdresser? How is someone like me, the son of a well-to-do family, to admit that his dream is to cut hair? My parents were dead set against the idea and forced me to take a law degree. They're dead now. I dream of scissors, of a salon with clients, bottles of shampoo and razors. I was born into the wrong family. It was a mistake. My whole life has been a mistake.

'A hairdresser? What on earth . . .' muttered Hubert as the doorbell rang.

He placed Léonard's diary face down on the Chesterfield sofa and opened the door to a blonde woman with a perm and piercing eyes, holding a pile of letters – the concierge.

'Léonard Larnaudie,' Hubert introduced himself. 'I'm back for a brief visit. Do you have post for me, Madame Martin?' he asked, more than a little proud of having remembered the concierge's name.

'No, I haven't had any for twenty-four years and you can smoke his cigars all you like, but if you're Léonard Larnaudie then I'm the Virgin Mary.'

Hubert did not react other than to say coolly, 'What makes you say that?'

'Oh, I can see you're a Larnaudie,' she said with a smile. 'I can tell from your eyes. But you're not Monsieur Léonard.'

There were footsteps and a breathless telegram boy appeared carrying a folded slip of blue paper.

'Where are you off to, son?' the concierge called across to him.

'To M'sieur Berthaud's place.'

'It's not here, it's the other staircase and he won't be home now. Give it to me and I'll slip it under his door.'

'Thanks, M'dame,' said the boy.

She turned to Hubert, who was still looking at her as the telegram boy went back downstairs, and shook her head.

'If you were Léonard,' she continued, smiling, 'you'd have had your eye on him, but you didn't.'

'I don't follow,' said Hubert.

'Just as I said, you're not Monsieur Léonard.'

Thinking on his feet, Hubert reached into his pocket, took out a one-thousand-franc note and held it out to her.

'Are we agreed that I had my eye on him?'

'Agreed, Monsieur,' the concierge sighed, snatching the note from his hand and departing hastily.

Hubert slammed the door. What was all this about eyeing up the telegram boy? He reconsidered the Greek alabaster torso and the Roman wrestler prints. He went back to the living room. The youths in their swimming trunks had still not taken a dip in the lake and the Greek shepherd on the clock was still staring blankly up at the ceiling. Hubert took a step backwards and sat down on the sofa. Cousin Léonard's bachelorhood could only have one possible explanation.

Thursday, 26 November 1930

Cousin André asked Madame Martin to pass on his invitation to Christmas dinner. I can't stand the concierge. She knows as well as I do who I really am. Nosy cow must have seen me out with Armand. I won't be going to my cousin's Christmas dinner. Besides, we've already planned to spend Christmas at the Cavalier Bleu with Jaimé and Eduardo who are planning to come dressed as Cleopatra and Nefertiti.

Friday, 27 November 1930

I've had an idea. More than that: a plan.

Armand said, 'Do you realise that if I hadn't brought you that telegram, we would never have met?' I was touched. I didn't mention that I often sent myself telegrams purely to catch a glance of the telegraph boys in their cycling trousers.

Since I met Armand, I've dropped my naughty habit. I love him.

Don't I?

Sunday, 29 November 1930
I bumped into André in the hallway. 'Still no wedding bells on the horizon, cousin?' he asked. 'Oh, there will be,' I replied. 'When I'm in Chile!' He stared hard at me and asked if I was serious. 'Deadly serious,' I replied and left.

The pages that followed contained hundreds of details about a hair salon Armand had scouted out on Rue de la Chaleille in the fifteenth arrondissement that he and Léonard were hoping to buy. They were trying to think of a name for it – Léonard was keen on La Marotte, after the hairdresser's mannequin, while Armand preferred Les Deux Ciseaux. It seemed that one night at the mysterious Cavalier Bleu, Cocteau – who must have been quite the regular – had plumped for La Marotte. Armand wanted Léonard to sell his apartment and use the money to buy La Marotte and the apartment above it, but in his diary, Léonard was adamant that this was not his 'plan'.

Wednesday, 2 December 1930
MY PLAN
Here it is. Here's how I'll get my own back and ensure the Larnaudies never forget me. I want to be a man

of mystery whose very name will conjure images of unattainable luxury and adventure for decades, no, generations to come. I shall become a legend even greater than Anatole – and my grandfather will help me from beyond the grave!

I'll take my few treasured possessions from the apartment, leave the rest and close the door behind me, never to return to 18 Rue Edgar-Charellier. Every day the sight of my closed shutters will remind my fellow residents of the smallness of their sad little lives.

I'll leave them to stew for a while and then, in five or six years' time, when Jaimé and Eduardo go to Santiago as they do every summer, I'll ask them to send a postcard I'll have written with these simple words: 'It's done!'

And then . . . I'll never be in touch again. They'll drive themselves mad wondering about my fortune and my life out there. They'll imagine me in haciendas, swimming in cool pools and biting into exotic fruits while giving orders to my armies of flunkies. I will for evermore be 'Léonard Larnaudie, the cousin who went to make his fortune in Chile and became so rich he can afford to leave his Parisian apartment empty'.

When in fact I'll simply be on the other side of town, at La Marotte, a place where no Larnaudie will ever set foot.

And all this will be possible thanks to Anatole's gold. Gold which doesn't belong to him, but from which the old miser profited handsomely. The old man's gold is mine! A good part of it, at least, for I could never carry it all. And this will be the final and most ingenious part of my revenge: the Larnaudies will never know what they're sleeping on . . . Sweet dreams, Larnaudies . . .

I am a genius.

Hubert choked on his cigar. 'Anatole's gold?' he blurted before catching his breath. 'What's this about sleeping on top of it?' he shouted into the empty apartment.

He shook as the words written twenty-four years earlier danced on the page before him. Reams of tedious notes on the salon followed before Léonard's last diary entry:

Wednesday, 9 December 1930
Adieu, Léonard's diary. You belong to another life. I'll burn you in the fireplace and close the apartment door behind me for ever. No sooner will the ink be dry than the flames will carry off my former life.
    Léonard Larnaudie, 5 p.m.

The remaining pages of the journal had been left blank. Hubert instinctively took his phone out of his jacket pocket to Google whether there was still a salon called La Marotte on Rue de la Chaleille. The inky-black screen displayed nothing more than the reflection of his own face.

She smiles enigmatically against a background of lakes and mountains. She smiles, her small hands resting in front of her, and you almost want to look behind you to see who on earth she is smiling at like that. Apparently, the sky was originally blue and her skin a pearly pink, yet now she is haloed in a sort of greenish gold mist. A soft mist with which people now associate her. It is said that the reason the smiling woman acquired that hue is that Leonardo mixed too much varnish into his paint colours.

Bob looked at Lisa Gherardini, known as the Mona Lisa. She was not behind bulletproof glass back in 1954. Nor was she lit by LED lighting developed by Toshiba specially for her, or guarded by two attendants, making sure the thousands of tourists who came to see her did not get too close. She simply hung in the gallery among all the other paintings. And, remarkably, Bob was one of the only visitors to the beautiful Florentine that afternoon. It must have been a special day for copyists because in front of almost every picture in the gallery, there was an artist perched on a stool at their easel, working, palette in hand, to produce perfect life-size reproductions. The Mona Lisa was no exception. A woman in her fifties in a blue smock was concentrating on her painting. She must have been coming here for weeks because there was already some varnish on her unfinished canvas and many details that she had reproduced with meticulous care. In two or three months she would undoubtedly have a very creditable copy of *La Gioconda*. With the tip of her sable brush, the artist was working on the light and shadow of the mountains. She was completely absorbed in her work and was probably miles away from the Louvre in spirit, in an imaginary valley and on the balcony of a house that had never existed other than in the imagination of Leonardo. As Bob looked at the painting, he told himself that the Mona Lisa was not smiling at some unknown person behind him, she was smiling at him, Bob Brown from Milwaukee. She was smiling at him with gentle complicity as if she had a message for him that could only be passed on by telepathy. Her hands placed calmly one on top of the other could almost have been mistaken for Goldie's. He had never noticed that before, although he and Goldie had looked together at the picture on the internet several times. You couldn't really imagine the Mona Lisa's hands rinsing beer glasses or carrying Bloody Marys on Sunday morning at the Why Not bar, and yet, they looked the same. Soft, with a wideish palm and long, slender fingers. Bob stood back. Yes, the Mona Lisa was definitely looking at him. And her eyes continued to follow him as he moved away.

Before coming to the most famous museum in the world, and regretting that he could not admire the pyramid that would not be built for at least another thirty years under the presidency of François Mitterrand, Bob had gone to the foot of the Eiffel Tower. At least that was the same as it would have been had he not gone back in time. He had removed his jacket so that his black leather HOG vest with its pins and embroidered badges was visible. His phone worryingly showed only one per cent battery but he smiled for a selfie. Bob in front of the Eiffel Tower in his Road Captain vest – the photo he would send to all his contacts from the Milwaukee Eagles Chapter, which hadn't been thought of yet. But his phone ran out of battery before he could take it. 'Fuck you,' groaned Bob, and some tourists turned to look at him. He sighed, put his jacket on again and slid the useless phone back into his pocket. He decided to wander along the Seine in the sun to reach the museum.

Afterwards, it was mainly his silent communion with La Gioconda that he remembered of his trip to the Louvre. The thousands of other paintings meant little to him. They were religious scenes whose meaning escaped him, epic battles he had never heard of, or Romans in togas and sandals. There were also portraits of famous men. Louis XIV was in coronation robes perched on shoes with red heels and ribbons, and wearing furs, lace and an improbable long, curly wig. He even had white silk stockings and garters. He looked more like a drag queen from a carnival float than a feared and powerful king. The museum, which was the size of ten chateaux put together, was so chock-full of paintings that Bob was not sorry to escape back into the fresh air and sun.

He crossed the square that housed the Comédie-Française and had to accept that he would not be able to see the Colonnes de Buren, highly recommended by his Cartoville guide – *Le Louvre et ses environs*. There was only a vast stone courtyard, instead of the striped columns where tourists liked to sit and take pictures of themselves. He walked through the Palais-Royal gardens and wandered through the streets before ending up in an arcade called Galerie Vivienne. The covered passages went in all directions with shops that were a little dusty but full of charm. One exit from the Galerie Vivienne led to a little square with a church and a blue-fronted shop called Au Cœur Immaculé de Marie. The window was full of various fonts, candles and religious pictures. Bob felt some drops on his neck – it was starting to rain. He turned towards the church and went to shelter under the porch. An old man sat at the top of the steps, a blanket over his knees and a dog at his feet. A cardboard sign propped against a cup with a picture of the Virgin Mary read, '14/18 war veteran – lonely widower with dog – thank you in advance.'

Can that be true? thought Bob. Then he reflected that the man certainly had a dog and looked lonely, so could well be a war veteran and why not a widower as well? There were men like that in the United States: Vietnam veterans who had lost everything and lived on charity on the streets. Bob thrust his hand into his pocket and held out one thousand francs. 'That's too much,' said the man. 'I know this is the Church of Miracles . . . but that's taking it quite far . . . Thank you, you're a prince among men and God will reward you.'

Bob gave him a friendly pat on the shoulder and stroked the dog. The rain was not easing off. A sign beside the church door read, 'The Basilica of Notre-Dame-des-Victoires contains throughout its interior more than 30,000 votive offerings, the biggest collection in the world. The atmosphere of contemplation in the basilica and the thousands of plaques giving thanks for miracles cannot but impress and move believers and casual visitors alike.'

Bob opened the door. The church was dimly lit by burning

candles. White marble plaques six by eight inches covered one wall, and another, and another. In fact, all the walls were the same. Arranged one above the other like a giant game of dominoes, the plaques went up the columns and even covered the arches. Bob looked slowly from right to left, and from top to bottom. There were hundreds, thousands, tens of thousands of white marble rectangles, each engraved with a sentence describing a particular miracle: 'I appealed to Mary when I was at death's door and she cured me completely.' 'N. D. des Victoires saved my two sons – 15 August 1866, Princesse St Elia.' 'My wishes have been granted. Thank you. 1931.' 'Thank you, Mary, for saving Gaston and Isabelle from the shipwreck of Parama.' 'I followed the Star of the Sea in my boat and arrived safely in harbour. Thank you. 1928.' 'Thank you for bringing me back Pierre, my husband before God. 1917. L. C.' 'He was lost but he came back to life. Thank you, N. D. des Victoires. Marie-Edwige Darcourt. 1904.'

'Thank you.' The words had been engraved in marble innumerable times. All these people could not have mistaken a simple coincidence or piece of good luck for divine intervention. Miracles must really happen here. Bob could picture himself ordering up a plaque and knew what it would say:

Thank you to N. D. des Victoires for bringing Goldie back to life.
Bob Brown from Milwaukee.
Wisconsin, USA, 2017.

A woman opened the red velvet confessional curtain, crossed herself and left the church. As Bob approached the confessional box he could make out the figure of the priest in the gloom behind the wooden grille. He sat down on the bench and drew the curtain. He could not see the priest's face behind the wooden lattice.

'I'm listening, my son . . .' said the priest softly.

'OK . . .' replied Bob, then quickly pulled himself together. 'I'm sorry,' he apologised, 'but my life is very strange at the moment.'

'You're American.'

'Yes.'

'And where are you from?'

'Milwaukee, slightly above the middle, to the right, near a big lake.'

'Lake Michigan,' said the priest.

'Oh, you know it?' said Bob, surprised. 'That's good; no one else here knows it. On our dollar, it says "in God we trust", but I don't believe in God; at least, it depends on the day . . .'

'And today, my son?'

Bob did not reply immediately. Then he said, 'Listen, if God does exist, he's all-seeing.'

'God sees everything, yes,' confirmed the priest.

'So he knows what is happening to me?'

There was a silence and Bob sighed. 'This is a church where miracles happen . . . *Je vouloir un miracle*,' Bob said, thinking his chances might be better if he made his request in French.

'*Je voudrais*,' corrected the priest.

'I'd like,' Bob started again, reverting to English, 'to go

back to my own time and for Goldie to recover and wake up. God has to give me my wife back. That's the miracle I'd like.' The priest did not reply and Bob looked down at his shoes. 'Do you think you could do something?'

'I'm going to pray for you . . . Bob.'

Bob paled. At that moment, the rain stopped and a ray of light came through the window, projecting blue and yellow reflections onto the confessional box. In the splashes of colour that glinted on the polished wood, the priest's seat was illuminated but there was no one there. Bob yanked open the curtain and rose to go.

'Monsieur!' a woman carrying copies of the next order of service called over to him. 'You can't sit there,' she said as she reached him. 'The confessional is closed,' she whispered. 'It's only open from 10 a.m. to 12 p.m., Tuesday and Thursday.'

Bob turned back to look at the confessional. It was empty.

The splash of liquorice liqueur dropped into the cocktail glass and slowly dissolved. Julien was taking advantage of a quiet moment in the afternoon to create a new cocktail. That's how Bloody Marys and Sidecars and so many other famous cocktails had come about: on a quiet afternoon, a barman had looked at the various bottles around him and come up with a strange but perfect mixture that no one had thought of before. Julien was trying to create a short drink with violet syrup as a base – a drink that would encapsulate Magalie. He would combine the syrup with vodka, gin and liquorice liqueur, and decorate it with the zest of a lemon cut like a shooting star, in honour of this being the year of the flying saucer.

Concentrating on his concoction, he thought about his brief telephone conversation with Professor Arpajon. He had used the telephone in the basement.

'Professor Arpajon, Charles Arpajon?'

'Professor Arpajon speaking,' the scientist had replied.

'Am I talking to the author of *Alien Visits and Space Phenomena?*'

There was a long silence on the other end of the line.

'How do you know about that? I'm still in the process of writing it.'

'I absolutely must speak to you,' begged Julien.

The scientist had agreed to meet him at seven o'clock that evening.

There was always a lull in the afternoon at Harry's Bar. The few customers sat nursing their drinks. It was Julien's favourite part of the day. Although today he was finding the fact that the decor had changed so little rather perturbing. The framed caricatures of Harry and the university pennants would be in exactly the same place on the wall sixty years later. Primo Carnera's boxing gloves would hang from the same spot on the ceiling, and the TRY OUR HOT-DOGS – CHIENS CHAUDS À TOUTE HEURE sign and the wall covered with foreign banknotes left by customers passing through would still be there too. Everything would be the same, in the manner of an embassy whose laws of operation had decreed that life inside would be timeless. The only difference was the absence of the Barack Obama sticker on the mirror and the talking Donald Trump puppet, and, obviously, his colleagues had been replaced by their 1954 counterparts. But, strangely, the team still consisted of an older man and a younger, one loquacious and one quiet, one large and one small, as if everything had to follow an established pattern of stereotypes. Even the customers complied with this rule: the same types of people were to be found in the same spot in the bar. As Monsieur Gérard, who had taught him his trade, said, 'A bar is an aquarium with its own ecosystem and particular species. Each fish is in its own place and nothing ever changes!' The reason the aquarium functioned so well was that everyone knew their role. So in the nook to the right of the bar, by the window,

Julien had served a whisky to a bored-looking man who was leafing through paperwork. Julien's new colleagues had told him that the man was a lawyer and spent his days in Harry's, which he had gradually come to use as his office. Sometimes his clients would phone him in the bar. Sixty years later, in the same place Julien would serve Mathieu, a bored-looking lawyer leafing through paperwork. Sometimes in the afternoon, Mathieu would pick up his mobile and speak to his clients, pretending he was in the office. Harry's was like a theatre where, as soon as a role became vacant, a man or woman would push the door open and step into it. This cycle would continue, come what may, across generations and death – and sometimes even beyond that. According to legend the ashes of a customer had been carefully hidden in a secret place – high up so that he could see the room. These had been his last wishes – to stay in the bar for ever. Julien looked up towards the place he was supposed to have been hidden and wondered whether the ashes were already there, or whether, now in 1954, the customer was still alive, perhaps even one of those present this afternoon.

Still thinking about how his new cocktail would turn out, Julien paid little attention to the couple who had come in and sat down at the bar. They were discussing the dress the woman would have to wear for the première of a film in New York in a few days. Her elegant companion smiled. 'Just two more fittings, Audrey, I promise.'

'I'm counting on you, Hubert. This film is important to me and it's also important to do justice to your creations,' replied the woman in delightfully accented French.

Julien turned to look, and froze. The young woman with the short hair and large eyes smiled at him and asked, 'What is that pretty purple drink?'

'It's something I'm trying,' stammered Julien, 'with violet syrup. But no one has tasted it yet.'

'I love that no one has tasted it yet!' enthused Audrey.

'I'll have one too,' said the elegant young man.

As Julien carefully prepared their cocktails, he listened discreetly and deduced that she had made a film, *Sabrina*, which took place in Paris and which was about to be released.

'What do you think?' asked Julien anxiously when she had taken two little sips.

'What do I think?' she repeated, looking doubtfully up at the ceiling before immediately looking at Julien. 'It's very, very good!' she declared, with a disarming smile. And Julien let out a sigh of relief.

'Mademoiselle is an actress,' said Hubert de Givenchy, winking conspiratorially.

Julien nodded and said, 'I've seen *Roman Holiday*.'

'He's seen *Roman Holiday*!' she said, turning to her friend.

'I have,' replied Julien, and almost added, and *Breakfast at Tiffany's*, before remembering that in 1954 Audrey Hepburn was still at the beginning of her career.

'It's a very subtle, feminine cocktail. Is there a hint of liquorice in it?' asked Hubert.

'Yes, just a splash, to make it purple and to offset the violet.'

Audrey asked what the cocktail was called.

'Abby,' he said, after a moment's thought.

'Abby? That's pretty. So I have drunk an Abby,' she said, delighted.

'A new cocktail?' asked one of his colleagues, coming behind the bar.

'Yes, with a violet base.'

'Write it down, Julien. Harry wants everything to be written down in the recipe book.' He tapped the large book on the bar.

Julien opened it and wrote in pencil:

Abby, short drink.
To a chilled mixing glass add: ice cubes, violet syrup (1 cl), vodka (4 cl), gin (4 cl).
Mix with a spoon, strain into a Martini glass. Pour a little liquorice liqueur down the side of the glass.
Decorate with a twist of lemon zest, cutting one end into a star shape and resting this on the rim of the glass.

The rain had stopped during the bus journey and sunlight reflected off the puddles. Hubert walked back up Rue de la Convention and counted four roads off to the right before Rue de la Chaleille. After leaving Rue Edgar-Charellier he had darted into the nearest café to find a telephone book. La Marotte – men's and women's hairstyling – was indeed located at 23 Rue de la Chaleille. As he approached, he saw the classic blue-and-red-striped cylinder hanging outside, as recognisable as the tobacconist's red sign. The prettily hand-drawn words LA MAROTTE – COIFFEUR POUR HOMMES ET FEMMES – BARBE ET COUPE arched across the window of a modestly sized salon. A line of meticulously polished hairdressing trophies stood at the bottom of the window. Hubert bent down to read the inscriptions: BEST HAIR COLOUR 1934 – TULLE FESTIVAL OF COLOUR, SECOND PRIZE GOLD CHIGNON – NICE 1950, DIAMOND MOUSTACHE – *ADAM MAGAZINE* PRIZE – DEAUVILLE 1937. There was also a framed black-and-white photo of a smiling man holding a pair of scissors beside the operetta singer Luis Mariano. The picture was autographed 'To Léo, the tenor of scissors . . .' Hubert peered into the salon. The man at work in the blue smock was the tenor of scissors himself.

He went in, walking into a haze of aftershave, hairspray

and soap. Antique china shaving bowls were artfully arranged on one wall and four red-and-white leather chairs that looked like American car seats, or a chic version of a dentist's chair, were placed in front of the mirrors. At the back of the shop were the shampoo area and an impressive fleet of moveable dryers whose Plexiglas hoods resembled the tips of explosive shells. The boss was working his magic on a young blonde's chignon.

'Just like that!' he said, twisting a lock of hair behind her neck. 'Look,' he said, picking up a mirror to show her. 'Here, it's elegant.' He nimbly combed back three locks of hair and piled them on top of her head. 'Here, it's limp, bland, tasteless.'

'If you say so, Monsieur Léo,' the young woman replied, smiling.

'I do, Mademoiselle Louise. It's your wedding, but my chignon!'

A blond man – could this be Armand? – began to walk towards Hubert, who told him he had come for a haircut.

'Very good, Monsieur,' the man said. 'And a shave too, perhaps?'

'Good idea,' replied Hubert. 'I'd like that gentleman to do my hair. He was recommended to me.'

'I see.'

The man went to whisper in Léonard's ear. The boss glanced over at Hubert.

'Could you possibly wait half an hour?' the first man asked. 'Take a seat, we've got plenty of copies of *Cinémonde*.'

Hubert put down his bag and opened the magazine, which was filled with news of Louis Jourdan's Hollywood exploits.

'Such a sweetie. She's getting married the day after

tomorrow,' Léonard said after the young woman had left the salon. 'I've known her since she was this high, haven't I, Armand?'

The fair-haired man nodded.

'So, what can we do for you? Come and take a seat in my office,' Léonard said, pointing to the chair.

Hubert sat down. Léonard stood behind him, ran two fingers along his cheeks and frowned.

'Do you use an electric razor?'

'Yes,' admitted Hubert. 'I ought to change the blade.'

'You should get rid of it, full stop,' sighed Léonard. 'They don't work, they cut badly and they're terribly noisy. And your hair?'

'It's too long,' Hubert guessed.

'I don't think so,' replied Léonard. They looked at one another in the mirror. 'You'd look like you were in the army if I took it too short. It's been very poorly cut, I must say,' he remarked, combing through Hubert's hair. 'Are you fond of your greys?'

'Not especially,' Hubert acknowledged.

'Let's cut them off then.'

'You're going to cut off the grey hair but not the black?'

'Yes. Hairdressing is a craft, Monsieur,' Léonard said seriously. 'Make yourself comfortable, put your head back and we'll start with the shave.'

He took a warm towel out of a box and gently passed it over Hubert's neck and cheeks. Next, he folded it into a triangle and left it just beneath Hubert's nose for a few seconds. Then he took away the towel and began massaging a mint pomade into Hubert's cheeks with his fingertips.

'Can you hear that scratching?' he said. 'See how badly those machines shave.'

Hubert nodded. He had to find a way to talk to him, but how? There were only two clients left in the salon, one sitting under the dryer and another whose hair Armand was doing while talking about *Hands Off the Loot*, a Jean Gabin film he had been to see half a dozen times. With a pot of soap and shaving brush in hand, Léonard spread a creamy mousse over Hubert's cheeks, neck and lips, making his mouth reappear with a swift stroke of the towel.

'Stay still,' said Léonard. In the mirror, Hubert watched him take a shining cut-throat razor out of his pocket and open it with a conjuror's sleight of hand.

The blade glided slowly over the skin, taking the hairs from one cheek and passing over to the other side, the chin and jaw before descending to the Adam's apple and slowly rising back up the neck. Hubert could restrain himself no longer.

'You're Léonard Larnaudie,' he said, and the blade came to a stop.

Hubert looked into the mirror and their eyes met. The image of the hairdresser holding the blade still against his throat hardly put Hubert at ease.

'I'm Hubert Larnaudie,' he gulped.

'Relax . . . Hubert,' murmured Léonard, 'and stop talking, or you might get cut.'

He finished the shave and picked up another warm towel, which he sprinkled with a few drops of another lotion and draped over Hubert's face. Under the towel, he breathed a scent of warm verbena and heard the bolt on the salon door slide across. Léonard must have signalled to Armand to shut the shop.

'I've come in friendship,' said Hubert.

'Can we be friends when we're part of the same family?' asked Léonard.

'I've brought a peace offering. Look inside my bag.'

He heard Léonard step away and open the zip. There was a pause.

'Where did you find this?' whispered Léonard.

'In your fireplace.'

'And what were you doing inside the apartment I haven't set foot in for twenty-four years?'

'I'm passing myself off as you.'

Léonard swept the towel aside.

'Hubert,' he said, 'I'm starting to like you. Come upstairs and tell me more.'

The stairs at the back of the salon led up to the apartment. They entered a room whose walls were lined with red fabric and covered in shelves of knick-knacks. Hubert sat in an armchair while Léonard took a bottle of Chartreuse and two glasses from a cupboard. 'I like the colour green,' he said.

'Me too.'

Léonard filled the glasses and sat down on a large cashmere-covered sofa. Sipping his liqueur, he flicked through the diary, nodding his head as he turned the pages. Occasionally, reading a certain phrase would bring a faint smile to his face. Then he closed the book and looked Hubert straight in the eye.

'So . . .' he said. 'What are you thinking?'

Hubert took a sip.

'May I?' he said, pointing to the diary. Léonard passed it to him. Hubert skipped over a few pages before stopping to read aloud:

'I will for evermore be "Léonard Larnaudie, the cousin who went to make his fortune in Chile".

And all this will be possible thanks to Anatole's gold. Gold which doesn't belong to him, but from which the old miser profited handsomely. The old man's gold is mine! A good part of it, at least, for I could never carry it all. And this will be the final and most ingenious part of my revenge: the Larnaudies will never know what they're sleeping on . . . Sweet dreams, Larnaudies . . .

I am a genius.'

After a silence, Léonard finally said, 'It's true. I am a genius.'

Hubert handed him the diary. 'Here, have it back – it's yours. I'll never tell anyone I met you – you have my word. But I want to understand.'

Léonard put the diary down beside him and paused. 'It's the monks' gold,' he said. 'Have you never wondered how Anatole was able to pay for a lift in 1911 out of his own pocket?'

'Yes, I must admit I have always asked myself that question.'

Léonard stood up and took something from the drawer of a small desk.

'Here's how,' he said, handing Hubert a large gold coin engraved with the profile of Louis XV. 'Number 18, Rue Edgar-Charellier is built on the ruins of Saint-Martin Abbey. Anatole's cellar leads to what was once the crypt. There's a trapdoor just beneath where he kept his wine. From there stone steps go down ten yards and a second, smaller staircase goes deeper still. At the bottom, there's a large empty room leading to a tunnel which takes you to the crypt – a large, vaulted space around the size of this room, where there are three chests filled with gold and jewels.'

Hubert listened, transfixed, as Léonard told him how he had come to discover Anatole's secret. When he was young, Léonard's bedroom window had looked out over the courtyard. Often finding himself unable to sleep – a problem that still plagued him in his fifties, he said – he would count the hours of darkness by the chimes of the mantel clock, sitting up reading or looking out of the window at the stars and the courtyard. Several times, on different days and at various hours of the night but always when everyone was asleep, he had seen light coming from the window of his grandfather's cellar and had begun to wonder why. The illustrated tales of crime he read in *L'Illustration* when no one was looking set him imagining secret societies, black masses, gatherings of villains and even ghosts with ball and chain.

One night, with butterflies in his stomach, he had decided to go down to the courtyard and look in through the window. He put his clothes on over his pyjamas and left the apartment as quietly as he could. He took the main stairs down to the courtyard and crept over to the lit window. He had a plan if the concierge spotted him – he would close his eyes, hold his arms out and pretend to be sleepwalking. Léonard was quick to point out what a feat of organisation and cunning this was for an eleven-year-old, talents which would only grow as the years went by. Peering in through the window, he was disappointed to find the cellar empty, but after a while he saw old Anatole emerging from a dark staircase that led up from deep below ground. He was holding a lantern in one hand, and in the other, two heavy-looking sacks which he placed down on a table with a muffled clink. He closed the trapdoor, brushed earth back over it and piled up a few old bits and pieces to hide all trace of his having been there. Léonard watched him put the lantern down on the table, delve inside one of the sacks and take out a handful of gold coins, letting them run through his fingers. Young Léonard's blood froze. The explanations he had imagined for the lit window were not so wild after all: Anatole really did have a stash of buried treasure. The sardonic smile on the old man's face would be etched on the youngster's memory for ever: a picture of Scrooge himself.

Not long afterwards during that summer of 1911, to the astonishment of the family council, Anatole would announce his intention to have a lift installed at his own expense. Nobody dared contradict the fearsome old patriarch and first inhabitant of the apartment block. Léonard could not say for sure whether Anatole had found the treasure during the building's construction in 1868, or in 1905 when, according to his parents, part of the cellar floor had caved in and had to be rebuilt.

'I think it's more likely he discovered it at that point,' Léonard concluded.

'And you never went down there before you left?'

'Not without the key!' Léonard retorted. 'The old man was nearly a hundred when he died! A year before I left. It was only when André moved into Anatole's apartment that the key became accessible. I took it during one of their endless Sunday lunches, digested to the sound of Bernadette murdering the piano.'

He refilled their glasses.

'Why didn't you take all of the gold?' Hubert pressed him.

Léonard smiled.

'It would take four men to carry one of those chests. Besides, you'll remember I wrote in my diary that I rather liked the idea of you all sleeping on top of the gold without the slightest idea it was there. So now you know everything,

Hubert. The treasure must still be there, if no one else has found it. Unless the cellar has been cleared out since.'

'Trust me, it hasn't,' muttered Hubert.

'Has André not noticed?' Léonard went on. 'I can see there's a family likeness but, still, can't he tell that you're not me?'

'No,' Hubert told him.

'God, there's no justice . . . They show their contempt not in what they say, but in how easily they forget. When they can't even remember what you look like, you realise how little notice they ever took of you,' Léonard said sadly. 'But, tell me, Hubert, why on earth are you passing yourself off as me?'

'It's a long story, Léonard. Let's just say I'm passing through. I don't really live here.'

Léonard nodded.

'We all have our secrets,' he said. 'So . . . tell them I've made a fortune in . . . vicuñas,' he went on more brightly.

'Vicuñas?'

'A small type of llama used to make cashmere. They're everywhere in Chile. Tell them I've got herds of thousands of them, lands as far as the eye can see and a hacienda with swimming pools.'

Hubert nodded. He didn't mention that he had already described the hacienda at length.

'Léo! Customers!' Armand shouted up from the bottom of the stairs.

'I'm counting on you not to destroy my legend, Hubert,' Léonard said sternly.

'I'll not only preserve it, I'll build it, Cousin Léonard, and I salute your tremendous chutzpah,' he said, raising his glass.

'Well, if a hairdresser doesn't have a talent for embellishment, he's in the wrong job,' said Léonard.

As the two men clinked glasses, Hubert concluded that Léonard might well be the nicest member of the family. They finished their drinks and Léonard walked ahead of Hubert to the stairs.

'I've one last question,' said Hubert.

'Fire away,' said Léonard.

'Did you really know Jean Cocteau?'

'Yes, of course. And we've stayed in touch. He's not very well. He had a heart attack and has gone down to Saint-Rémy-de-Provence to recover,' replied Léonard. 'I had a letter from him just last week. You'll never guess what he's hooked on.'

'What?' asked Hubert, following Léonard downstairs.

'Flying saucers! It's all the press can talk about. Just a little thing, between you and me,' Léonard said, turning round. 'Don't cut your hair, not even the greys. You look great as you are – tall, dark and handsome.'

'The years 2017 ... 1978 ... 1954,' Professor Arpajon said, drawing out the words.

Julien had been sitting in the scientist's office for twenty minutes. On one side of the room there was a large blackboard covered in figures and equations while the remaining walls held dark wooden shelves filled with hundreds of coloured leather-bound volumes, all on the same theme: astronomy. Arpajon was an authority on the subject and his studies of meteors had been seminal works for the last forty years.

The professor didn't know it yet, but the work he was putting together on the current wave of flying-saucer sightings would do a great deal of harm to his reputation. His usual publishers would turn him down and he would be forced to self-publish. As soon as the book came out, he would be ridiculed by many of his colleagues, who would spread the rumour that the eminent space expert was suffering from senile dementia. Some would even use the opportunity to prevent him being elected president of the Academy of Sciences two years later.

When Julien had rung the bell of the apartment, an elderly housekeeper had come to the door and invited him to sit down in the hall. Half an hour later she passed him again.

'Are you still here?' she exclaimed. 'Come with me.'

She marched Julien to the door of Arpajon's office and knocked hard.

'Professor! You've forgotten your visitor!'

Arpajon came straight to the door, apologising for having lost track of time. He looked exactly like the black-and-white author photo on the inside back cover of the book he was yet to finish: a man of almost seventy-five with longish white hair wearing pince-nez and a white coat over a smart waistcoat. Notoriously absent-minded, Professor Arpajon had missed countless trains, planes and boats on his travels around the world in search of meteorites, from the deserts of Libya to the Siberia of Tsar Nicholas II – but on the plus side, his poor timekeeping had kept him from travelling in his first-class cabin aboard the *Titanic*. As the ocean liner set off from its stopover in Cherbourg, Charles Arpajon was sitting on a café terrace writing the eighteenth draft of a lecture on the theories of late-eighteenth-century scientist Pierre-Simon Laplace, who suggested that meteorites might originate from volcanoes on the Moon. At ten past ten that night, the world's largest transatlantic liner was casting off towards its tragic fate. At quarter to eleven, Charles Arpajon looked up from his notes and realised he was the last customer in the café, and the Americans would not be hearing his lecture any time soon.

'How do you know the working title of my book, young man?' he asked as he welcomed Julien in, looking slightly flustered. It had been a long time since he had mixed with anyone other than his colleagues, whose average age was in the mid-sixties. At the scientist's invitation, Julien took the seat opposite him at the desk, feeling equally ill at ease.

Arpajon might not believe a word of his story. What if he sent him away, or called the police?

Julien took a deep breath and began: "'Chapter 8: They don't travel through space, but through time. Having journeyed to all four corners of the globe in search of meteorites of all shapes and sizes, thereby amassing considerable knowledge of the subject, I can say with some certainty that if intelligent alien lifeforms have visited our planet, they have travelled not through space – as meteorites do – but through time. What we know as flying saucers are in fact, as I will go on to demonstrate, time machines.'"

Arpajon's jaw dropped as Julien recited from memory from the book he had bought for a fortune off eBay.

'But . . . who are you?' Arpajon asked breathlessly. 'I wrote that page word for word eight days ago and nobody's read it. Have you been to my house?' he said, looking increasingly worried.

'No, Professor,' Julien replied calmly. 'But I want to go home to mine, and I think you can help me get there.'

'And where is home, for you?'

'Ask me instead "when" it is.' Faced with the other man's silence, Julien launched in: 'I come from the year 2017 . . . Your theory is correct, Professor: UFOs travel through the corridors of time.'

Julien went on to explain about the evening at Hubert's apartment, the bottle of wine they had uncorked and how they had woken up in 1954, not forgetting the disappearance of Mr Flying Saucer who had drunk the same wine and seen a UFO above the vines.

'The years 2017 . . . 1978 . . . 1954,' Arpajon murmured

again. 'My God, I like being proved right, but if what you say is true, son, you've just opened a doorway . . .' he said, rising to his feet. 'More than that!' he went on, suddenly carried away. 'A great wall has been knocked down; a labyrinth razed to the ground!'

He picked up a sponge and wiped all the notes off the blackboard. All that remained were a few constellations of chalk, like stars in the dark sky.

'Space,' muttered Arpajon, 'and time,' he went on, drawing a horizontal line in chalk. Then he marked three points at uneven intervals on the line and wrote the three dates above. 'When did your great-grandfather see the flying saucer above the vines?'

'On 16 September 1954, just before midnight.'

'And it's the fifteenth, today and you arrived this morning. So you're a little less than two days ahead of this contraption flying over the vines. And the people who drank this wine in 1954 thought it uncommonly good, but didn't go back in time?'

'I don't know anything about that. I only know that my great-grandfather disappeared with his dog after drinking the wine in 1978.'

'But why did the dog disappear too? The dog didn't drink the wine. That's the theory shot!' Arpajon complained.

'But that's the thing – she did drink it,' Julien admitted. 'Ausweis used to lap up wine. They poured some into the water in her bowl.'

'So the theory is right,' Arpajon went on. 'But why the devil did the drinkers in 1954 stay put, while you've come back two days ahead of time?' he sighed, perching on a stool.

Silence descended, broken only by the clock ticking on the mantelpiece.

'I can't help you, son,' the professor sighed. 'Even though your presence here is irrefutable proof of my theory: these craft travel not through space, but through time. I don't want to know anything about the future, but I doubt you've found life on other planets.'

'We haven't,' Julien confirmed.

'That doesn't surprise me, and your telescopes must be a damn sight more powerful than ours . . . That doesn't mean they don't exist, only that they're too far away. We don't know what fuel these spaceships run on, but we do know that it contaminated the Saint-Antoine grapes. How and why, we'll never know. Wine and time.'

Arpajon stood up to write these words in capital letters on the board.

'That's the equation. What is the relationship between wine and time?'

Arpajon returned to his stool.

'I'm thinking . . . the ageing process?' Julien suggested after a pause.

Arpajon thought for a moment. 'Ageing?' he said, turning to his blackboard as if he could see equations taking shape on it. 'Why yes, that's it. That's the key. The longer the wine is aged, the further back in time you go. Do you see?'

Julien looked blank.

'Yes!' Arpajon cried, bounding to his feet. 'The 1954 drinkers didn't go anywhere because the wine was a Beaujolais Nouveau – it hadn't been given the time to age! You drank the bottle sixty-three years after it was harvested and you're just under two days ahead of the flying saucer. As for your great-grandfather, he drank it in 1978, which is twenty-four years after the harvest . . . both of you have been sent back to the same space-time: 1954. The space–time continuum is broken when the flying saucer goes over the vines. If sixty-three years put you ahead by two days . . . then your grandfather's twenty-four will put him only . . . eighteen hours and thirty minutes ahead of the flying saucer, and if my theory is right and if you go to Beaujolais tomorrow, my boy, you should find Mr Flying Saucer from 1978 there, and for him, the change will happen around . . .'

He took out a pocket watch and closed his eyes to make a quick calculation.

'. . . around five thirty in the morning. Like you, he won't realise what's happened until he leaves his house. The only trouble is, he won't go unnoticed in the village,' said Arpajon with a look of concern.

'Why's that?' asked Julien.

'Because there will be two of him! The Pierre Chauveau of 1954 – who'll see his flying saucer tomorrow night – and the other Pierre who's twenty-four years older and set to arrive from 1978. You and your friends don't have this problem, because you weren't born in 1954, but he will.'

'What do I have to do, Professor?'

'Let's go to Beaujolais. I'll come with you. You must find your great-grandfather from 1978 and go to the vineyard with him and your friends at the exact moment the flying saucer appeared. The spaceship's arrival should set everything straight again. Your great-grandfather and his dog will go back to where they came from, in 1978, and you and your friends will return to 2017.'

Then he turned to the window whose light was now flooding the room and whispered gravely, 'We have to go back and close the door that has been opened on the corridors of time.'

That evening Bernadette Larnaudie's piano playing was a particular torture for her husband, who could not help exchanging pained looks with his guests.

Magalie, Bob and Julien had gathered in Léonard's apartment beforehand, and Hubert gave a quick explanation of how the dinner should go. He did not mention his encounter with Léonard or the revelation of the monks' treasure, but explained that he would say he had made his fortune in vicuña wool. If they backed up his story of lands as far as the eye could see, herds of vicuñas, the magnificent hacienda and the swimming pool fed by hot spring water, everything would be fine.

But when Julien began to describe his meeting with Professor Arpajon, they all paid more attention because what he had to say seemed more important than Hubert's tedious vicuña story. Julien provided everyone with a train ticket for early the next morning. They would meet Charles Arpajon on the platform and take the train into Beaujolais for their encounter that evening with the UFO. The professor had said that was their only hope for returning to their own time.

During the meal, Abby and Julien threw themselves into tales of the endearing little vicuñas they liked to pet in the pastures. They recalled the day they had brought an injured fawn down from the plateau and how they had cared for it and kept it as a mascot at the hacienda. Hubert kept clearing his throat to make them stop. But in vain. He had to admit that their descriptions had captured the attention of Bernadette and André Larnaudie. André declared that his cousin had become the Rockefeller of vicuña, and seemed delighted with his own turn of phrase.

Bob introduced himself as a serious businessman. He promoted himself by claiming to be chairman and president of Harley-Davidson. Hubert noticed how much they all enjoyed taking on a persona that was quite different from their own for the space of an evening. Gone were the property director of Sofreg, the barman, the china restorer and the motorbike engine designer. They had slipped into their new roles with astonishing ease. The strangest and most confusing part for Julien and Magalie was pretending to be married.

'You must be dying of hunger,' apologised André Larnaudie when the last plate of charcuterie had been finished. 'Cousin, why don't you all go and have supper at Les Halles?'

'Oh, yes, Les Halles!' exclaimed Magalie.

Hubert looked round at the others and as they all seemed so keen, he agreed. His grandfather recommended Au Veau qui Tète, a brasserie he considered even better than the more famous Au Pied de Cochon. As they were all getting their coats on in the hall, André Larnaudie drew Hubert aside. 'Dear cousin,' he began seriously, 'you are a man of the world, far more than we are, the Larnaudies of 18 Rue Edgar-Charellier. I have some shares in the Suez Canal and I was thinking of buying more, despite the problems in Egypt. I am betting that the English will keep hold of the canal, and Westerners will be there for ever. What do you think?' he finished proudly.

'I wouldn't do that,' counselled Hubert. 'The canal will be nationalised by the Egyptians in two years and your shares will be worthless. Sell them all, tomorrow morning.'

'Are you sure, cousin? I'm very surprised by what you say.'

'Certain!' said Hubert firmly.

The taxi dropped them at the corner of Rue Montmartre and Rue Rambuteau. They took a few steps and then stopped to marvel at what they saw in the lamplight.

'Amazing . . .' murmured Julien.

The renowned Baltard pavilions of Les Halles rose up in front of Saint-Eustache Church. Built under Napoleon III, the ten identical glass halls built side by side covered a huge area right in the centre of the city. They would be razed to the ground fourteen years later to make way for the modern shopping centre, and the food market would be moved to an outer suburb, depriving Parisians for ever of the sight that now greeted them.

'Mind your back! Watch out!' and Hubert stepped smartly out of the way, avoiding a trolley piled with crates of vegetables that almost ran over his foot.

All around them men in caps, cigarettes at the corners of their mouths, were pushing handcarts teetering with impressive piles of crates overflowing with provisions. Crates were also piled on the ground in front of the stallholders, whose cries cut through the general commotion of the nocturnal buyers. In the distance they could see the triangular marquee between pavilion 5 and pavilion 6 and the circular marquee opposite, which marked the entrance to Les Halles. How on earth were they going to find Au Veau qui Tète in that maelstrom? Trying to control his panic and desire to turn tail, Hubert announced gloomily, 'Émile Zola used to call this the belly of Paris . . .'

'The belly of Paris,' repeated Bob, impressed.

'Move over, mate!' cried an impatient voice and Julien stood aside to let a cart heaped with a good dozen deer go by.

The animals were tumbled one on top of the other, as if they had all succumbed to a sudden deep slumber. How could one man manoeuvre all that by himself through the crowd? It must weigh at least a ton.

'Can someone help me here, damn it?'

A sort of tramp appeared to guide him with great gesticulations.

'Make way for the deer! Make way for the deer!' he called, forging a passage for the cart.

The noise of barrows on the cobbles – a metallic rattle which seemed to fill the air entirely – was starting to become oppressive.

'Butchers! Stop thief!' cried a voice and the commotion stopped for a second and then immediately started up again.

'Butchers! *Louchébems!* Butchers coming through,' called the voice again.

Four burly butchers in bloodstained white aprons appeared from nowhere and sliced through the crowd, all carrying knives with blades longer than their forearms. Magalie moved closer to Julien.

'Where did he get to?' yelled the first butcher.

'Here!' shouted a porter carrying crates, and in the crowd a man was running in a panic hither and thither, nudged out of the way by the elbow or foot of those pushing barrows, like a pinball.

As the gang of butchers bore down on him, blades drawn, the man left a bag on the ground and fled towards Saint-Eustache Church. The first butcher bent down and picked up the fine black leather bag and brandished it over his head like a trophy. Then his broad face flushed and broke into a grin. 'That's a rich lady's bag, that is!' and he burst out laughing. His fellow butchers followed suit. As he passed in front of Magalie, the butcher looked at her and said loudly, 'She'll be back for it tomorrow. We'll keep it safe for her. Meat porters! Meat porters!' he yelled, throwing his head back.

A large man with a cap and a moustache came out of a bistro. 'The meat porters aren't here! But I used to be one.'

The butcher went over and held out the leather bag. 'Old friend, give this to your mates; the owner will come and collect it tomorrow.' Except he spoke in slang and was answered in kind, '*Lercimuche louchébem, lomptequem sur loimique.*'

'What's he saying?' asked Bob, bewildered.

'It's the slang used by butchers at Les Halles,' Hubert explained. 'Louchébem, a made-up language only used here. He said he would see to it.'

The large man, still holding the bag, caught sight of Hubert. 'It's my neighbour, Monsieur . . . Larnaudie!' He came over, smiling. 'Marcel Bouvier, formerly a meat porter at Les Halles, originally from the Auvergne and your new *charcutier-traiteur*, remember me?'

'Yes, of course, Monsieur Bouvier,' said Hubert, shaking his hand.

'You've come to visit Les Halles?'

'Apparently so,' replied Hubert, sounding a little apprehensive.

'Have you been before?' asked Bouvier.

'Yes, but not in these . . .' murmured Hubert, looking at the pavilions. 'We're trying to find Au Veau qui Tète.'

'That's on the other side, Monsieur. Would you like me to take you there? And I could show you and your friends round Les Halles?'

'I don't want you to go to any trouble, Monsieur Bouvier,' said Hubert politely.

'It's no trouble, Monsieur Larnaudie! It would be a pleasure,' replied Bouvier. He half-opened the door of the bistro, letting out a blast of accordion music. 'I'll be back. Look after my drink and this too!' and he slung the bag onto the bar where it was caught like a rugby ball by a waiter. 'Let's go!' he said, rubbing his hands together. They all followed him through pyramids of cauliflowers that were stacked on the pavement like miniature Towers of Babel.

'Hello there!' Bouvier greeted a little old man sitting on a stool in front of an enormous open suitcase.

'That's Père la Souris,' Bouvier told them. 'He's here every evening selling buttons, laces and scarves. He's been here for ever. I think they built Les Halles around him. What have you got this evening, Père la Souris?'

'I have these new leather laces. Very good quality,' croaked the old man.

'We're going right here,' said Bouvier, and the little troop turned off to go into the fish hall. 'We'll cut through fish. From all over, and all fresh.'

He stopped and looked at them. 'Take a look about, ladies and gentlemen; this has been my whole life!' He spread his arms wide and then they all set off again at a trot through the building. 'Hello, Maurice,' he said to a porter.

'Hello, Marcel,' replied the other man.

Julien looked up at the iron pillars supporting the vaulted ceiling. Hubert also stared up at the girders and the walkways all around that looked, with their lamps, like covered streets.

'I was a meat porter at Les Halles for twenty-six years,' said Bouvier. 'I left my village when I was only sixteen. When I arrived in Paris I had a paper round, I was a labourer, a removal man, and then one day I said, "Why not be a porter at Les Halles?" And I passed the exam.'

'There's an exam?' asked Bob.

'Of course! You need to be strong, clever and . . . hard working,' replied Bouvier. 'And you have to be able to read, write and count – Hello, Fernand! – so there's a test like the school leaving certificate. You must be French, with a clean criminal record and have done your military service – Hey there, Antoine – you also have to be at least five foot five and you have to succeed in the challenge.'

'What is the challenge?' This time it was Julien who asked.

'You have to be able to carry a load of Paris paving stones weighing thirty-two stone for sixty yards without putting it down.'

'Thirty-two stone?' repeated Hubert.

Bouvier shrugged. 'A cow weighs more than that, Monsieur Larnaudie.' Hubert imagined his new charcutier hefting cattle as easily as if they were made of paper. 'It's only if you can do all that that you get to wear the smock and the big leather hat, the *coltin*, the hat of market porters,' said Bouvier, indicating with his hands around his head the enormous size of the hat worn by members of his guild. 'Inside the hat, there's a lead lining which helps you carry things and protects your neck. Left now,' he said, and they turned down a new alley.

Around them, fish were arriving in their hundreds on slabs. 'Where are my whiting?' barked one fishmonger.

'In the Channel!' cried another.

'I'll knock you into the Channel if you're not careful,' responded the fishmonger.

There were mackerel, sole, trout, skate, red mullet, turbot, squid, octopus and scorpion fish all around them. A huge man wearing the wide porter's hat was carrying a swordfish on his back that was even bigger than he was. The pointed bill of the fish rose like an antenna above his hat.

They continued on past the various stalls.

Pyramids of oysters and halved tuna fish the size of dolphins were displayed side by side with lobsters and crayfish that were still alive and crawling over each other. It was as if someone had emptied the Atlantic into the night. Magalie wondered if she was dreaming. Was that really a little live seal she saw, sitting on a heap of crushed ice? A man was throwing it a red ball and the animal caught it on its nose before making it bounce several times.

'There's a seal,' she said to Bouvier.

'Yes, that's Betty,' he replied as if it were completely normal.

'Lou-lou-lou Louchébems!' cried Bouvier, entering the meat hall.

'Oh, it's you, l'Auvergnat,' replied the butchers, smiling as they chopped meat, with open bottles of wine on their blocks.

The group passed in front of them and one of the butchers planted the sharp blade of his knife into his block. '*La lollijem lillefic*,' he declared, looking wide-eyed at Magalie.

'What does *la lollijem* mean?' Magalie asked Bouvier.

'It means pretty girl.' Bouvier was smiling. 'Come on, we're nearly at Le Veau,' he said, leading them towards the exit. One of the butchers called something after them in Les Halles dialect.

'You'll see some high society in Le Veau,' Bouvier said, knowingly. 'Hello, Prosper,' he greeted another porter passing by.

'*Salut l'Auvergnat*,' replied Prosper as he disappeared into the night.

Bouvier opened the door of Au Veau qui Tète, letting Magalie, then Hubert, Julien and Bob pass in front of him.

The restaurant was enormous, with opaline lights hanging from the steel roof frame. There were tables for two or four interspersed with much larger ones that could accommodate parties of a dozen or more. There was a lively hum of conversation and waiters' exclamations but each table had a beautiful white cloth, sparkling glassware and bottles in silver buckets. It was an interesting mix of informality and Parisian chic that Hubert had never experienced before.

'Marcel! Get back to work,' the manager shouted from behind the bar where elegantly attired men and women crowded alongside butchers in stained aprons and others less easy to identify, in caps and beautiful scarves, who were quite openly counting fat bundles of money.

'I've brought some friends,' Bouvier said to the manager, who looked horrified.

'I'm full up, I can't fit in any more.'

Bouvier was disappointed. 'But they've come a long way; one has come all the way from America! What about that big table over there?'

'Do you see who that is?' said the manager, with a knowing

look. 'La Môme's friends have all gone off to the Alhambra, but I can't put people at their table!'

At that moment a solid but surprisingly nimble-looking man signalled solemnly to Marcel Bouvier, who whispered to Hubert, 'Follow me,' and removed his cap as they made their way to the table.

'My dear Marcel, how are you?' boomed a voice well known to Parisians because they had heard it so often at the cinema.

Jean Gabin wore a grey suit that matched his silver hair, and a pearl-coloured tie with a coordinating pocket handkerchief. By his side a brunette, whose black dress skimmed her delicate shoulders, ran her hand through her short wavy hair. Her brown eyes fell on Magalie, who could not believe that she was looking at Édith Piaf and smiled back at her.

'I'm well, Gabin,' said Bouvier, shaking his hand.

'There's no need to introduce Édith.'

'Madame Piaf, it's an honour to meet you,' said Bouvier as Julien and Hubert nodded in astonished silence.

'How do you two know each other?' asked Piaf, finishing her champagne.

'Oh, we've known each other for so long it's lost in the mists of time, isn't it, Marcel? We sold newspapers together one summer, when we were, what, sixteen, and then one day I spotted Marcel under a side of beef – he'd become a porter at Les Halles.'

'And Gabin . . . had become Gabin!' finished Marcel Bouvier.

'And how's your charcuterie coming on?'

'Nearly ready,' said Bouvier proudly.

'I hope I'll get an invitation to the opening. You're here with friends?'

'I showed them how to get here, but there are no tables.'

The star of *La Grande Illusion* looked around the restaurant. 'There's room at our table. Édith?' He turned to the singer.

'Yes, of course, sit down!' said she. 'We're having bœuf bourguignon – do you like that?'

They nodded.

'Four more bourguignons – and two bottles of bubbly!' Gabin told the manager.

'I'm going back to my friends. I'll leave you now, Monsieur Larnaudie,' said Bouvier, putting his large hands on Hubert's shoulders.

He went off as a waiter laid their places and Magalie sat down beside Édith Piaf.

'So, my friends, what do you all do?' asked Gabin, serving them champagne. His blue eyes rested on Hubert, who could not reply. He was still wondering if he might not have gone mad, or suffered a serious mental illness. Maybe he was about to wake up in a hospital bed, or in a straitjacket with doctors looking suspiciously at him and telling him it was terminal.

Bob came to his aid. 'I'm Bob, Bob Brown. I'm American, I've seen your films and I work for Harley-Davidson.'

'Oh yes, the motorbikes I've seen in America. I don't know America well, apart from Hollywood.'

Hubert watched them talking. He found the way the American addressed the 1950s actor with such ease especially disorientating. It must be the Hollywood effect. Maybe watching so many series and films with implausible plot lines meant that people could accept the most unimaginable scenarios and nothing would surprise them.

'At Harry's Bar, owned by Harry MacElhone? Yes, I know it; I went there once with Marlene,' he heard Gabin say to Julien, who had just explained where he worked.

'And Mademoiselle?' asked Gabin.

'She is a china restorer,' replied Édith Piaf.

'And what about you?'

'I look after property, asset management.'

The actor nodded.

'I didn't know that you two knew each other,' said Magalie, indicating Piaf and Gabin.

'We don't really. I was dining with my producer and Édith was with her friends and when they all left, Édith and I decided to finish our champagne together. That's the magic of Les Halles . . .' explained the *Port of Shadows* actor.

'He's a good guy,' said Édith Piaf, putting her hand on Gabin's shoulder. 'And he's handsome, which is even better.'

'Oh, please,' said Gabin in mock annoyance.

Piaf winked at Magalie and whispered to her, 'Yours is also handsome.'

'Mine?'

'The barman. You two are the youngest at the table; don't tell me you don't fancy him.'

'I don't know,' said Magalie, narrowing her eyes to look at Julien.

'But I do,' said Piaf.

Everyone declared the bourguignon delicious, and by then the bottles of champagne were almost empty. Magalie and Julien were now sitting beside each other and Piaf was answering

Bob's questions about 'La Vie en Rose' and advising him to listen to the records of one of her protégés who was just starting out, Charles Aznavour. Gabin leaned towards Hubert.

'Tell me, Monsieur Larnaudie, since you are in property, if I have understood correctly: is now a good time to sell?'

'Don't sell now, don't sell anything,' said Hubert. 'But everything will start getting better in 1966.'

'1966?' Gabin was staggered. 'You must be a magician – a man who can predict the market twelve years in advance!'

Piaf leaned towards Gabin and whispered to him, 'We have to make sure these two young people kiss before the evening's out, understood?'

'Understood, la Môme,' murmured Gabin.

'I would like to go and look at the stars. Are you coming, Magalie?'

'Good idea, that,' agreed Gabin. 'I'll come and have a smoke outside with you. Do you want to come with us, Julien?'

Magalie got up to follow Édith Piaf, and Gabin and Julien followed suit.

Outside there were a few handcarts passing, but the bustle of earlier had calmed down. Above the streetlamps you could see a few faint spots of light across the night sky.

'I'm not sure I have ever seen the Great Bear,' said Magalie.

'Just there, on the right,' said Piaf, 'but you can only see a bit of it, just the bear's leg.'

A few yards away, Jean Gabin was offering Julien a Gauloise, after having taken one for himself. His lighter flared. They both lit up, and Gabin exhaled in the glow of the street-lamp. 'I like this time,' he said, 'when the vegetable porters are taking their break. There's a little moment of calm.'

Julien was nodding his agreement when Gabin said, 'So, young man, what are you waiting for to kiss your sweetheart? Can't you see that she's expecting you to?'

'Gabin,' murmured Julien.

'"Gabin, Gabin,"' echoed the actor, nodding gently. 'That's very nice but I'm not the one who interests you; that would be Mademoiselle Magalie.'

Magalie was gazing at the stars as Piaf silently retreated beneath the awning of the restaurant.

'Sweet dreams,' murmured the actor, blowing a cloud of cigarette smoke.

And he in turn melted back into the shadow with Piaf. She placed a finger on her lips and they both watched Julien and Magalie walking slowly towards each other.

'I'm going to join my friends at the Alhambra,' said Piaf softly. 'Do you want to come with me?'

'I'll come, la Môme.'

Julien's heart was thumping so hard he couldn't hear any of the noises around him. What he had hardly dared dream of was about to come true. Now here they were together in the silence of the night in that state of intoxication that precedes a first kiss. You know that it is going to happen and that it will seal a love that needs no words. It was inevitable, just a matter of seconds away. Something minute would be the signal: a gesture, a blink, the light in their eyes.

'Julien . . .' murmured Magalie, and in response, Julien whispered Magalie's name.

Then they came together and their lips met eagerly. Breathlessly, they closed their eyes to abandon themselves to a wave of pleasure that overpowered everything else. The more they kissed, the more they felt as if they would never be able to stop. It was like finally being able to drink from a forbidden source, a source you could thrillingly hold tight. And it felt as if their desire was lighting up the night. Julien could feel Magalie's hips against his body and the lamp post digging in to his back. They got their breath back and hugged each other, staggering slightly. Julien, his head buried in Magalie's neck, murmured her name several times. When he looked up, he saw that the hotel in front of them was called Hôtel du Paradis.

They returned briefly to the restaurant to tell Bob and Hubert not to worry, that they were going for a walk but would meet them the next morning in time for the train.

'That's love,' commented Bob when they had gone out again.

'Do you think so?' said Hubert incredulously.

Bob nodded, thinking of Goldie sleeping in limbo on the other side of the world, and in another era. *'Je vouloir un miracle,'* he murmured to himself, and finished his glass of champagne.

In the hotel bedroom, they fell onto the bed and Julian began to undo the buttons on Magalie's dress one by one, and to kiss her neck all the way down to her breasts. Under her left breast, he discovered her heart was guarded by the tattoo of a curled-up cat.

'I'll explain,' she said, running her hands through his hair.

As Magalie and Julien made passionate love on the bed in the cheap hotel, which for once was living up to its name, Hubert was asking the waiter for the bill, only to be told that Monsieur Gabin had taken care of it.

A burst of steam hissed between the wheels as Magalie climbed onto the train. She turned to kiss Julien, who was waiting for Professor Arpajon on the platform. In the corridor, she squeezed past passengers standing at the windows, smoking or chatting in little groups, and opened the sliding door to the six-person compartment where Bob and Hubert had already taken their seats. A large woman pulled her knitting out of a wicker basket, two needles stuck firmly into the wool.

'Not exactly the height of comfort,' said Hubert to Magalie as she joined them. 'Even a second-class TGV seat would be a vast improvement on this.'

The compartment had black-and-white pictures captioned simply 'Scenes of France', depicting lakes, mountains and the odd flock of sheep. Aside from that the decoration was perfunctory, with brown imitation-leather banquettes as hard as bare wood and luggage nets hanging above their heads. It occurred to Magalie that neither she nor Hubert, Bob or Julien had bags to put there, nor had they booked return tickets or anywhere to stay. They were embarking on a one-way journey, banking on the old scientist's theory being correct.

'He's not coming!' shouted Julien.

Magalie stepped out into the corridor and pulled down the

window to find Julien pacing up and down the platform. The stationmaster of the Gare de Lyon blew his whistle and shouted, 'All aboard!'

'Get on, Julien,' Magalie said and he reluctantly obeyed.

Standing beside Magalie at the window, he leaned out as the wheels began to turn. At the end of the platform, they could see Arpajon running towards them carrying a travel bag.

'Professor!' Julien cried. Arpajon stopped, breathless, and flung his arms up in surrender as the train pulled away.

Outside the windows of the compartment, the countryside unfolded to the gentle click of knitting needles. Arpajon's empty seat had been taken by a large, round-faced man in his fifties with slicked-back hair and tinted spectacles, who was reading the paper. He was smoking a cigarillo, tapping the ash into the ashtray on his armrest at regular intervals. He pretended not to notice Magalie waving the smoke away several times, and anyway, everyone smoked everywhere, and they were perfectly within their rights to do so. With the exception of a few wind turbines and nuclear power stations, Hubert thought the landscape reassuringly similar to how it looked in 2017, with fields, woods, power lines and isolated buildings that made you wonder who could live there, so far away from everything.

Bob leaned over to read the title of the article on the back of the man's newspaper: 'Ten Years of Votes for Women'.

'Couldn't French women vote?' he asked Hubert.

'Not until General de Gaulle passed an order in 1944,' he replied.

The man lowered his newspaper, looked at Hubert and then returned to his reading.

'It was 1920 for us, I think,' Bob said.

'It's crazy they had to wait until 1944 here,' said Magalie.

The man lowered his paper again. 'Not really,' he said snidely. 'There was a time when people wondered if they even had a soul.'

'That's a myth,' Hubert protested.

'Not at all,' the man retorted. 'It was a theological issue.'

'It's a myth,' Hubert insisted, 'linked to an inaccurate record of the Council of Mâcon in the sixth century.'

The man shrugged.

'Tell me, Monsieur,' the large woman snapped, pausing in her knitting. 'I do hope you're not giving the question serious consideration.'

He looked at her, raising his eyebrows.

'Whether women have souls, or are equipped to have their say in a country's political decisions? When I see how you choose to spend your time,' he said, nodding at her knitting, 'I must say I have my doubts.'

'You're very rude, Monsieur!' the woman exclaimed. 'If women like me didn't spend their time knitting, where do you think your socks would come from? And what, may I ask, is your own favourite occupation?'

'The German Occupation,' he replied smoothly, taking a last puff on his cigarillo and letting the smoke out between his teeth.

The woman nearly choked with rage.

'I'll have you know, Monsieur, that my husband was a communist and member of the Resistance. He was deported and has a posthumous medal for bravery. Men like him died for France's honour.'

The man calmly stubbed out his cigarillo and looked round the compartment, smiling to himself.

'A communist's wife . . . an American . . . a Gaullist,' he went on, staring at Hubert. 'Don't try to deny it, it's obvious you're hoping he'll return to office. And you?' he spat at Magalie.

'A feminist?' she said with a cheeky smile.

The man looked at her with disdain as if to say, 'I knew it', then tilted his chin questioningly at Julien.

'Me? A bit like all of them: feminist, Gaullist, communist, American, barman . . .'

'Unbelievable!' the man muttered.

There was a silence and then Magalie leaned in to him.

'You know,' she said, 'the right to vote is only the beginning. There's also going to be a pill that will let women have sex without getting pregnant, divorce on the grounds of the husband being at fault, and the right to have an abortion.'

'And we're going to have a black president of the United States,' Bob added.

'And there'll be same-sex marriages,' threw in Julien.

'And a woman will lead Germany,' Hubert concluded.

The man flushed scarlet, stood up, retrieved his suitcase from the overhead net and walked out, slamming the door of the compartment behind him.

'Good riddance!' exclaimed the large woman. 'Men like that are good for nothing but shovelling muck. They forget a woman bore them, wiped their bottom and taught them to hold a fork.'

She went back to her knitting with tears in her eyes.

The incident over, everyone retreated into their own

thoughts. Bob was thinking that 1954 in the USA may have meant colourful jukeboxes, chrome-plated cars and the first Elvis tracks, but it was also a time when black Americans couldn't sit with white passengers on buses. Magalie was reflecting on the condition of women and came to the same conclusion as her grandmother: that things would begin to improve when a pretty blonde girl called Brigitte Bardot began turning heads and dancing barefoot on tables. Julien was looking at this from a different perspective: a girl like Magalie – with gothic leanings, financially independent and living her life the way she wanted – was simply inconceivable in 1954. As for Hubert, he was beginning to think he recognised the man they had argued with from documentaries and books on the Second World War, a well-known '*collabo*' who had fallen off the radar after the Liberation, but he couldn't for the life of him put a name to the face.

The woman put down her knitting needles and took a saucisson, a slab of pâté, a loaf of bread, a knife, two bottles of milk and some cups out of her basket.

'Help yourselves,' she said.

Julien poured out glasses of milk while Bob cut slices of saucisson and they all enjoyed an impromptu rustic breakfast. The woman knew Charmally-les-Vignes well and invited them to come with her when they got off the train. Her brother-in-law was coming to pick her up in his truck and could drop them off on their way. Julien looked at his watch – it was almost 9 a.m. If the author of *Alien Visits and Space Phenomena* was not mistaken, Mr Flying Saucer and his dog Ausweis had returned to 1954 from 1978.

There were plenty of customers drinking bowls of coffee or, in some cases, large glasses of red wine at Charmally-les-Vignes's sole café-bar, L'Auberge de la Belette Rouge. At the bar, two men in flat caps were silently playing the dice game 421, cigarettes in their mouths, while others discussed the harvests that would start in three days. The talk was of grapes, sun and fermentation.

'Same again, please, Marie,' one of them asked the landlady, a rather hunched woman with short hair and glasses.

She uncorked a bottle of red and was beginning to pour when the door opened with a crash that made them all start.

'I saw Chauveau!' cried the small ruddy-faced man in the doorway. 'He's aged twenty-five years, by God. His hair's white and he's covered in wrinkles! He looked at me as if I was a ghost and didn't even say hello. And he had a different dog! It wasn't Sieg.'

Everyone stared at him, their glasses suspended in mid-air.

'You're going mad, Riri!' the landlady cried. 'You drink like a fish, and soon you'll be seeing lizards in your bed like Aimé Lagrange!'

'I'm not mad and I'm not drunk, damn it!' the man said, stamping his foot. 'And I'm not going to end up like Aimé.'

'But Chauveau was just here!' The woman banged the

counter for emphasis. 'And he hasn't changed since yesterday and he had Sieg with him, you damned fool!'

'Where's he gone?' the man shouted.

'Now?' said the landlady. 'A hundred yards down the road, probably!'

Riri ran out of the café and down the road. From behind, he saw the figure of a man walking with a grey German shepherd towards the church. He drew level, grabbed him by the shoulders and turned him round so abruptly that the dog jumped up and bared its fangs.

'What the hell . . . you're the same as yesterday!' he exclaimed when he saw his face.

'What's the matter with you, Riri?' said Pierre Chauveau, pulling himself free. 'You're going to get yourself bitten. You know Sieg's an Alsatian, don't you? You should give up the bottle, Riri, or you're going to end up like Aimé.'

'God must be punishing me,' shouted Riri, moving away and making the sign of the cross. 'Holy water's what I need. I'll have to make do with the fountain,' he cried, striding off towards the stone fountain and dunking his entire head under the cold water.

'Come on, Sieg. We don't need to see this,' said Pierre Chauveau, and he walked off with his dog.

Everyone at La Belette Rouge was now talking about Riri. They listed those who had fallen on Bacchus's battlefield like the soldiers named on the village war memorial, noting that the grape had claimed almost as many lives as enemy fire had done. They spoke of Aimé Lagrange, who saw reptiles between his sheets and ended up dying of a heart attack one stormy night; Old Queuvillard, the gamekeeper, who would go to the woods at full moon to 'honour the fairies' until the day he hanged himself from a sturdy oak branch; Claude Fourquel, discovered at the bottom of his well after weeks of claiming to hear a woman's voice calling from there; Vincent Pignard, nicknamed 'Vincent the Strong', a bearded giant who, after a night of heavy drinking, had decided to take on a group of rutting wild boar with his bare hands; Émile Chabert, known as 'just a drop', who had ended up paraplegic and senile and for the last fifteen years of his life repeated one single phrase: 'I'll have just a drop more.' The names and anecdotes kept coming and the conversation was still focused on these colourful characters when the newsagent came in.

'Morning, everyone!'

'Hi, Pierrot,' the men replied.

'Small white, please, Marie,' he said, resting his elbows on the bar. 'I've just seen Chauveau. What's happened to him? He's aged like a bunch of old grapes. I saw him looking at a newspaper outside my shop but he didn't buy it – scurried off like a rabbit.'

'And I suppose he had someone else's dog with him?' said the landlady sarcastically. 'Am I surrounded by alcoholics? You're as bad as Riri. I'll stop serving the whole drunken lot of you if this goes on any longer. You're lucky we don't have a war coming. Much good you old soaks would be at defending the country. Nothing but woodworms making your way through the barrels.'

Pierrot didn't argue. 'I was only saying . . .' He shrugged. He picked up his glass and opened the newspaper to read a story about a flying saucer that had been spotted in Auvergne.

*

The wind whipped their faces. The red Renault pick-up truck flew along the road as the sun broke through the clouds. All four of them were standing in the back of the truck, clinging to the bar that ran behind the cabin. Magalie smiled and rested her head on Julien's shoulder.

'We'll get there,' he said, as her black, violet-scented hair touched his face. 'By midnight we'll all be home again.'

'I hope you lovebirds are right,' Hubert smiled.

'Look left!' shouted Julien. 'It's the castle of Robert le Rouge. Apparently the duke's treasure is still there.'

As they turned to look at the towers silhouetted by the sun, Hubert remembered that if they made it home, he too would soon have a date with chests of gold.

Mr Flying Saucer was sitting against the wall of a mountain refuge at the very top of the hill. The refuge, built several centuries earlier at the spot known as Le Saut-du-Loup, was used as a shelter for shepherds and walkers who had lost their way in storms. He knew the place well, having come here to reflect on every major decision of his life: his marriage to Mélanie, buying Claude Pierret's land, reroofing his house and even the operation to fix his slipped disc. Only surrounded by the peace and quiet of nature could he really think things through. With his spent pipe in his mouth and Ausweis lying at his feet, he was whittling a piece of wood with his pocket knife, nodding his head as he worked.

'The flying saucer's what made the wine turn, isn't it, Ausweis? That's why we're here – because we both drank it,' he said aloud as the dog whistled in its sleep.

Pierre had clocked sooner than the city-dwellers that something was wrong that morning. The night before, after knocking back the bottle of Château Saint-Antoine 1954 and pouring a good splash into his dog's bowl as usual, he had gone to bed with his head full of images from *Close Encounters of the Third Kind*.

At first nothing had seemed out of the ordinary. He and his wife had had breakfast and then he had put on his coat, lit his pipe and taken Ausweis to the door, only to find it was raining.

'Foul weather,' he grumbled.

He noticed something was different on the way to the winemakers' cooperative. The weather had brightened up and it was now quite warm, one of those lovely September days that feel like the height of summer. Perfect weather for grapes, he said to himself; if only the weather had got its act together before now, with only three days to go before the harvest.

Skirting the vineyards, he and Ausweis stopped at the well where locals used to collect their water before they had taps at home. As a child, he would go there regularly – even after dark, when it scared the wits out of him. The well had fallen into disrepair and had long since been filled in, but today it stood there stubbornly, like a mirage, with its wrought-iron roof and pulley. Chauveau puffed on his pipe, walked a little way into the vines and bent down to pick a grape. He bit into it. It tasted nothing like the one he had tried yesterday. Ausweis barked as the postman came cycling down the dirt track and turned onto the road to the village. He called out, 'Good morning to you!' as he passed. Chauveau watched him go without saying a word.

That was Martial the postman, all right. No doubt about it. Only Martial had retired years ago and, by 1978, was well past riding a bike, let alone putting on his uniform and doing the rounds. With the dog following close behind, Chauveau took a few steps down the road towards the shelter where the bus stopped three times a day. He saw an old-fashioned aqua-coloured Renault bus pull in and pick up a girl and a man. It drove off and silence descended again. Chauveau walked over to the bus stop and the seasonal timetable caught his eye. It listed bus times for this autumn . . . of 1954. Chauveau glanced over at the well and then returned to the timetable.

'Ausweis,' he murmured. 'Something's happened. We've gone back in time, girl. Come quickly!' And he strode off towards the village.

All appeared normal as they entered Charmally and he briefly felt reassured until he bumped into Riri on a side road. The two men looked at one another with mutual horror. Then Chauveau upped his pace and turned off to the left without a backward glance. It had been over ten years since he and the rest of the village had attended the funeral of Rigobert Barratier, Riri for short. Since then, they had visited the cemetery every 6 November – the date of his death – to lay the first bottle of every new vintage at his gravestone. Outside Pierrot Marqueuil's newsagents, he picked up a newspaper from the pile: the date on today's *Le Progrès* was 16 September 1954. Through the window, he glimpsed Pierrot standing at the till, turning his way. He put down the paper and ran, just catching the tinkling of the shop bell and Pierrot shouting, 'Chauveau? Is that you?' as he went.

When he reached the house he had left less than an hour earlier, Pierre Chauveau saw himself – or rather, himself as he was twenty-four years ago – through the kitchen window, talking to his wife Mélanie, herself twenty-four years younger.

'Holy cowpats,' he muttered. He saw himself go out into the courtyard and attach Sieg to a lead that was hooked to the wall before heading back inside. He could only hear snippets of the conversation from inside the kitchen in which he was saying that Riri was going to end up like Aimé Lagrange, and Mélanie replied, 'No surprise there.' Straining at the lead, Sieg reared up at the gate and Mr Flying Saucer walked over.

'Good dog, Sieg,' he said to the Alsatian, who was staring at him in astonishment. Sieg poked his nose through the fencing to get closer to Ausweis, his descendant, and began whining and running around in circles before leaping up at his master.

'Calm now, Sieg,' he said.

But the dog, who had been abandoned by the SS ten years earlier, was in no mood to calm down, barking furiously and almost strangling himself pulling on his lead. Mr Flying Saucer could hear more yapping from inside — that must be Schnell, Sieg's daughter and the future mother of Ausweis.

'Stop that racket, the pair of you!' Pierre Chauveau yelled from inside the house, and Mr Flying Saucer made himself scarce.

'Come, Ausweis. We need to have a think. A very serious think,' he said to the dog. 'Let's go up the hill.'

And off they went towards Le Saut-du-Loup.

The piece of wood had become a figure the size of a chess piece and with the tip of his knife Mr Flying Saucer was now carving him a grape-picker's basket. Concentrating on his work, he continued to order his thoughts out loud: 'Tonight's the night the blasted flying saucer's going to fly over. If we went back to the same place, maybe when it was all lit up we'd be sent back home . . . What do you think, girl?'

As he was asking this question, three miles down the hill the leather lead that Sieg had been madly yanking broke loose, pulling off the hook and a chunk of the wall itself with it. The dog jumped the gate and made for the main road as fast as his four legs would carry him.

As the truck pulled into the village square, it had to swerve to avoid a dog that ran out in front of it and sped off up the hill. Everyone clung to the bar as the vehicle jolted before pulling over.

'All right back there?' the driver shouted out of the window. 'Bloody hell,' he said, stepping down from the cabin. 'That looked like a wolf on a lead!'

'Sieg . . .' murmured Julien, gazing after the four-legged form that was now no more than a dot on the horizon, veering off the road into the forest.

When they walked through the door of La Belette Rouge, everyone turned to look at the four unfamiliar faces before returning to their conversations. The group chose a table and sat down. Before they could order anything, the landlady came over and set down a lovely oval carafe and four glasses, just as a bearded man with a wide-brimmed black hat opened the door. He nodded to the men at the bar, who returned the gesture.

'I hear Riri's been having visions?' he said to the landlady as he took off his hat and hung it up.

'And Pierrot too, Monsieur le Maire,' she sighed. 'They've both seen Chauveau as an old man with a different dog.'

Magalie, Julien, Bob and Hubert exchanged glances.

'How disappointing!' laughed the mayor. 'They could have dreamed up something far more outlandish. Who was it who used to see fairies?'

'Old Queuvillard,' a man shouted out.

'That was it,' the mayor went on. 'Altogether more amusing than the sight of a wrinkly old Chauveau.'

'And you remember what happened to him?' the landlady asked him.

'Yes,' he mumbled, going off to talk harvests with the men at the bar.

'He's here,' Julien whispered. 'He's come back.'

They all stared at each other in silence.

'Your scientist's theory is correct,' Hubert said, gravely.

'And there are two of him in one place: the forty-seven-year-old and the seventy-one-year-old,' Julien went on.

Magalie poured out the wine and they clinked glasses.

'What would you do if you returned to your village, having gone back in time twenty-four years?' asked Julien after taking a sip.

They thought about this for a few seconds.

'The same thing I did yesterday morning,' Hubert suggested. 'I'd start by going home.'

'. . . to find yourself already there, but twenty-four years younger,' Magalie carried on.

'And if you realised you'd gone back in time and there were two of you in the same place?' Julien continued.

'I'd fear I'd lost my mind,' said Hubert, downing the remainder of his drink.

'I'd probably turn to drugs,' suggested Magalie.

'I'd go into the forest on my own to think,' said Bob.

Julien went quiet, then his face froze and he put his glass down on the table.

'To Le Saut-du-Loup,' he murmured. 'That's where he went whenever he needed to make a decision. It's a mountain refuge up on the hill. That's where Sieg was going – he's gone to find him!'

He leapt to his feet and bounded over to the bar.

'Excuse me, Madame. Is Le Saut-du-Loup far from here?'

'Not very, son,' the landlady replied. 'Just keep going straight out of here, then cut through the forest until you get to the old dovecote and it'll be on your left. It's steep, mind – you'll need a good pair of shoes.'

Hubert's Weston moccasins slipped on the grass and he had to cling to a tree stump before Bob set him back on his feet. Further on, Julien held out his hand to help Magalie up. At last they all reached a flat path leading into the trees, through which you could make out an old drystone building with a tiled roof worn down by rain. Julien stopped and the others followed suit. An elderly man was sitting on the grass with his back to the wall, flanked by two big German shepherds with lolling tongues, one dog grey, the other beige. The knife blade was just rounding off the hat of the little grape-picker model when the two dogs pricked up their ears and Mr Flying Saucer looked up. Using one hand to shield his eyes from the sun, he made out four figures, one of whom had just broken off from the group and was walking slowly towards him. As Julien came closer, he felt as if he was approaching a hermit or old sage after a long journey fraught with hazards.

The four of them had truly been on a voyage of discovery to find themselves here before the old winegrower, watched over by his faithful hounds, an oracle of the forests.

'You're Pierre Chauveau,' Julien said, kneeling down beside him. 'I'm Julien Chauveau, son of Michel Chauveau. I was born in 1986,' he went on softly, 'and you're my great-grandfather.'

Pierre eyed him with suspicion.

'That dog's Ausweis and this must be Sieg, the one the Germans left behind. I come from the year 2017. My friends and I drank a bottle of Château Saint-Antoine 1954. Just like you did yesterday . . .' Julien went on. 'When the flying saucer flew over, it changed the Saint-Antoine wine and since then whoever drinks it will go back to 1954. It's been proven by an eminent scientist.'

Pierre continued to stare at him.

'If we all head to the vineyard tonight at the same time the flying saucer appeared, we should all go back to where we came from. My friends and I to 2017 and you and Ausweis to 1978.'

The old man, who had not taken his eyes off Julien, raised his chin.

'Come on, son. What kind of a fool do you take your great-grandfather for?' he said.

'Excuse me?' mumbled Julien.

'I don't need an expert to tell me I've come back to 1954. I'm perfectly capable of reading the date in the newspaper. And you bet I'll be standing under those twinkly lights tonight because that's where all the trouble started. Never seen the like . . .' he muttered, clambering to his feet. 'Come on then!'

he said, placing his hand behind Julien's neck. 'Say hello to your old great-grandad.'

And Mr Flying Saucer put his arms around him as the two dogs stood to greet Magalie, Bob and Hubert.

Hubert, having immediately been nicknamed 'the Parisian', had launched into his usual explanation about where he lived, in the apartment block built by his ancestors. Again, this seemed to carry weight with Mr Flying Saucer, who said approvingly, 'That's good; you're following in your family's footsteps.' Magalie was designated 'la Belle' and Bob, predictably, 'the American'.

Pierre wondered aloud what they would eat, since they would be stuck on the hill until evening. Then he announced that he would set traps and they could eat rabbit.

'You mean you'll skin them and roast them on a spit?'

'Yes.'

'Oh no, not for me,' demurred Hubert. He explained that he never ate rabbit because they looked too much like cats, at which Pierre rolled his eyes.

'What do you want to eat, Parisian? Trout?'

'Yes, I'd like that!'

'Some people are so fussy,' complained Chauveau.

He went into the refuge in search of fishing rods. But although the building, with its large iron grill in the stone fireplace and the logs handily stacked beside it, provided everything for a reasonably comfortable night sheltering from a storm, there was nothing at all that you could use for catching fish.

'But there used to be fishing rods here! Nothing much else, but fishing gear at least,' Chauveau complained. Meanwhile, Julien was looking at a 1944 calendar that had been left on a sideboard. Then he noticed some photochromes of village scenes. The framed prints were hung on the walls in an attempt at decoration, as if to make the large room seem more homely. There were also mattresses piled in a corner and copper saucepans. 'People have lived here?' asked Julien. 'I thought it was just a refuge.'

Pierre didn't answer. Julien picked/up the newspapers that lay on the dusty floor. They were also from 1944.

'Right,' said his great-grandfather, 'we'll have to make our own fishing rods,' and he went back outside. He eyed the badges on Bob's leather Harley-Davidson vest. 'How much do your badges mean to you, American? I could use them as hooks.' Bob took them off and held them out to the winegrower.

'We'll go and cut some rods in the forest, and we can make our own flies. It's the lines that will be tricky. We could make them with reeds, but I doubt they would dry in time for tonight.'

Magalie put her hand into her pocket and took out the reel of golden thread she had bought at Odette's. Pierre took the reel from her to assess the thickness of the thread. 'She's full of surprises, la Belle!' he said, pinching her cheek. 'Come on, follow me, we'll go and fish in the Galante.'

And they went into the forest, followed by Sieg and Ausweis. Pierre and Julien led the way, and the dogs brought up the rear.

'I've heard so much about you,' Julien said to Pierre.

'Because of the flying saucer? Everyone made fun of me. I'd have been better off saying nothing about it. But you'll see tonight whether or not I was making it up.'

Then Julien brought his great-grandfather up to date with who was who in the family and who had had children. He did not say that his parents had left Charmally-les-Vignes and that no one lived there any more. But Pierre Chauveau wasn't interested in the future anyway. The few things Julien did say about 2017 left him sceptical. Especially the use of smart-phones. Julien tried to explain, 'You telephone people to let them know you've arrived somewhere.'

'What for? People can see when you've arrived, can't they?'

'You can take photos and send them to friends. For example, you could take a photo of a deer in the forest.'

'What for? Everyone knows what a deer looks like.'

'It's to share what's going on in the world.'

'Don't people meet up in bistros and read newspapers at the bar any more?'

Pierre kept producing common-sense objections that Julien found hard to counter. 'What happened during the war in the refuge at Le Saut-du-Loup?'

'You're very curious . . . But I also think nothing gets past you, and that's reassuring. It's a refuge, so it's logical that people would take refuge there, wouldn't you say?'

There was a silence between them, then Pierre shrugged, saying, 'I can't see any harm in telling you. That's where we hid the Rosenblums.'

'The Rosenblums? You hid a Jewish family?'

Pierre nodded. 'With my father, yes. But it wasn't only us, the whole village knew about it.'

'But no one ever told me that,' said Julien, dismayed.

'Of course not. Why would they have?' asked his great-grandfather, stung. 'People didn't talk about these things; it wasn't anyone else's business. We told the Germans they were local people from the hills; we taught them some phrases of patois, so that the Krauts couldn't understand what they said, and they left them alone. They were completely taken in,' he finished with a smile.

'And you never told your children about it?'

Pierre shook his head. 'It was all a long time ago.' And Julien understood that no more would be said on the matter.

Instead Pierre went over to a bush, opened his knife and began to cut five long branches into slim, supple rods that he distributed to everyone.

The light filtered through the autumn leaves that also littered the ground. There was every hue from yellow to red through burnt terracotta and ochre. How would they be able to find their way through the maze of trees which all looked the same? As did the thousands of leaves on the ground. There were no points of reference. Hubert was starting to doubt they would ever reach a river, so endless did the forest appear. Mr Flying Saucer stopped and looked all around at the treetops.

'What are you looking for?' asked Julien.

'A nest. We need feathers.'

He cupped his hands round his mouth and produced a bird call, then stopped to listen. An answering call rang out. 'Follow me.' He repeated the exercise several yards further on. This time the answering call was very near. 'It must be here,' and he looked up. High above them in the branches, a bird poked its head out of a nest and looked at them. 'Where there's a nest, there are feathers. Here we go,' he said, bending down to the base of the trunk. 'We can make flies with these.'

They stopped to fix their lines to the rods. Mr Flying Saucer cut the feathers into triangles to make the flies and attached them with the safety pins he had removed from Bob's badges. Then they went up a little embankment and discovered the Galante river shimmering in the sun. Rays of light filtered through the branches and danced on the crystalline water as it flowed between shining stones. At the bends in the river, deep ponds had formed between the rocks.

'La Belle,' said Pierre, and Magalie went over to him. 'You and your fiancé should stand on the large stone there; Parisian, here,' indicating a rock, 'and, American, you go opposite. I'm going into the water. On my signal, cast your lines.'

Everyone took up their allotted position and the dogs stood vigil on the highest rock. Above them, some birds flew off as Pierre waded into the water until it was mid-thigh.

'Cold?' asked Hubert.

'Certainly is.' Pierre smiled, his fishing fly clenched between his teeth. 'But it doesn't matter.' He froze. 'Quiet, everyone!'

Hubert had crouched down on his rock. Bob, opposite, was studying the reflections on the water while Magalie and Julien stood together, their fishing rods poised, holding the flies in readiness.

'There are some real beauties,' murmured Mr Flying

Saucer. 'Back in 1954 they were big. We're going to have a feast.'

Then he removed the fly from his mouth and flung his arm backwards. The golden thread arced through the air until the fly landed far off on the surface of the water. 'Now, everyone!'

Bob cast his line, and everyone else followed suit.

'I'm not sure if—' began Hubert.

'No talking,' Pierre Chauveau cut him off. 'Your voice vibrates on the water. Do you think the fish are deaf?' They all stayed silent, lulled by the murmur of the flowing river, the birdsong and the wind in the trees.

The bucolic scene seemed far removed from the city and the world and they all felt as though they had found the essence of life: humans were not meant to sit in an office chair answering emails, or checking their bank accounts on a screen, or reading about world events on their phones. Humans had lived for millennia in nature, experiencing its beauty, taming it and taking from it the resources needed for survival, as other species did. Building shelter, hunting, fishing and sewing, they had taken their place in the spherical ecosystem spinning in nothingness that we call Earth. At some point, it had all become rather complicated. We had followed causes, developed aspirations, started wars, and decided that technical advances would lead humanity to great heights. And so the mad rush for progress had begun.

Hubert thought of the old fishing rods he had seen in the cellar, just as his own almost leapt out of his hands. He managed to keep hold of it. 'It's pulling,' he shouted, panic-stricken.

'Wind the line round your hand!' Pierre responded. 'Since we don't have reels.'

'Got one!' said Bob, leaning on his rock.

'It's pulling a lot!' cried Hubert, standing up.

'Of course! These aren't sardines,' said Pierre, who had hooked a fish and was drawing it towards the river bank.

'I have one!' said Julien

'So do I!' said Magalie.

Then they all moved backwards winding in their lines. Finally Hubert's trout cleared the water and he saw it, about the size of a half-baguette, dancing on the end of his line. Hubert knew that the image would be one of the most beautiful he would ever see and he suddenly felt cut off from his life before. Rue Edgar-Charellier, the management committee, the burgled cellars, the cracks the tunnelling of line 14 might make, the lift and even Anatole's gold all seemed irrelevant. All that mattered was this fishing party in the sun with friends, and the gleaming fish they were going to share. He had never felt so alive.

Back at the refuge, the winegrower arranged dried leaves and logs to make a fire. Hubert helped him bring out the wrought-iron grill and place it on top. They found cutlery in the drawer of a table. Pierre then lit the leaves with his flameless cigarette lighter and asked Julien and Magalie to blow on them. The fire ignited easily and everyone waited for the first embers then placed their fish to roast on the bars that were turning orange in the heat. As the trout were gently cooking, they discussed the bizarre things that had happened to them. Bob told them about his encounter with the priest in the church. He had asked for a miracle for Goldie, only to discover the priest was no longer there. Magalie, Hubert and Julien were at a loss to come up with an explanation.

'Perhaps he wasn't a priest?' suggested Pierre, finishing off sculpting his little grape-picker.

'Then who was he?' Bob asked.

The winegrower didn't reply. With a flick of his knife he completed the shoes, thereby putting the finishing touches to his perfect little wooden figure. 'My father showed me how to do this,' he told Magalie, who was looking at the little carving. 'And he learned from his father, who made deer as well. I can't do that; I find the hooves difficult. But it passes the time,' he concluded, turning the fish on the grill one by one with the point of his knife.

They declared the fish delicious, imbued with the flavour of the woodland herbs Pierre had gathered on their way back. They passed round the only cup they had found inside, having filled it from a bucket fed by a hose pipe that carried spring water down to the refuge. Then they fell asleep. Magalie was the first to drop off, snuggled in Julien's arms, then Hubert dozed off and Bob had stretched out on the grass, using his jacket as a pillow. A little way off Ausweis and Sieg shared the remains of the trout. Only Pierre Chauveau stayed awake, sitting by the fire lost in thought as the sun set. He turned to look at Magalie sleeping, the pretty girl who had come back from the future with her strange black clothes, her strapless dress with the red cat, and the boots with buckles. He put his hand in his pocket and took out the little grape-picker. He looked at it in the firelight then slipped it into Magalie's pocket.

'Since you like it, la Belle, I'm giving it to you,' he murmured and Magalie stirred without waking.

Sieg came over and pressed his nose against the old man's shoulder. 'You're going to have to go back,' he said and the dog looked straight at him. 'You have to go home now, Sieg.'

The dog continued to stare at him, then turned towards Ausweis who was a few yards away, unmoving. She came towards Sieg and the two of them sat down in front of Pierre, imploring him with their eyes.

'No,' said Mr Flying Saucer, 'you have to go, Sieg,' and he leaned over his dog, stroking his neck. 'Go now!' he said commandingly, and stood up.

The dog went a few steps, turned to his master and then to Ausweis, who whimpered.

'Be quiet, Ausweis,' said Mr Flying Saucer, and Sieg lowered his head and disappeared into the night.

A good minute passed before the howling of the Alsatian could be heard from the bottom of the hill. It seemed to pierce the night all the way up to the moon, like a heart-rending cry from the beginning of time. Then it was drowned out by the church bell sounding eleven o'clock at night. Mr Flying Saucer threw the remains of their pail of spring water over the embers. 'Wake up, everyone, time to go!'

They went down the hill by the light of the moon, sometimes having to feel their way or hold on to the shoulders of the person in front when the trees overshadowed the route. Then they walked for a while along paths, watched suspiciously by owls and other nocturnal feathered creatures that hooted briefly to warn others of the passage of the unexpected little group. Eventually the forest opened onto the vineyards and Ausweis began to run. In the black of night, the tortuous, dark vines looked like mandrakes. Far in the distance, they could make out the towers of Robert le Rouge's castle. They stood out against the clouds made iridescent by the gibbous moon.

They crossed several vineyards to reach the Saint-Antoine plot.

'Here we are, right on time,' said Pierre. 'All we have to do now is wait.'

They looked around. There was no noise any more as they crouched down among the vines. Bob pulled a grape off. 'You mustn't eat it,' said Julien, worried.

'We still can, at this hour,' said Pierre. 'You should try them; they're very good this year.' And they all took a grape.

It was eleven fifty when the sound of footsteps made them all turn to look at the road. A figure was approaching. Pierre

Chauveau was the first to stand up to see himself entering the vineyard twenty-four years earlier. Bob, Hubert, Julien and Magalie stood also. Now the figure was coming towards them through the vines.

Pierre said soberly, 'It's going to happen any minute.'

And they all watched in silence as the Pierre from twenty-four years ago drew ever nearer.

'Good grief, it's Sieg!' said Mr Flying Saucer, seeing his Alsatian come flying down a row of vines and stopping in front of him. He was immediately welcomed by Ausweis, who buried her face in her ancestor's neck. 'But you can't stay here, Sieg; you'll go back to the future,' said Mr Flying Saucer despairingly.

'Look!' said Magalie. Then she murmured, 'The stars . . . are moving.'

They all looked up at the sky. 'They're not stars,' said Julien.

'Oh . . . my . . . gosh,' breathed Bob.

Something huge and silent was manoeuvring into position above Jules Beauchamps's vines. Julien was open-mouthed. All the research he had read since adolescence, which took up eight bookshelves in his apartment, had started and culminated in this moment: he had now entered the very small circle of those who are never believed, but have seen with their own eyes.

'There it is . . .' murmured Mr Flying Saucer, and Magalie slipped her hand into Julien's and held it tight.

'*Mon Dieu*,' whispered Hubert, as the Pierre of 1954 stood frozen, staring up at the sky.

He stayed that way for a while, and then the object above

was flooded with light. They saw him cover his face with his hands then fall backwards.

The vineyard was plunged into bright, blue-sky daylight. The light intensified, radiating through the air, and Julien crouched down to put his arm round Pierre's shoulder, and his great-grandfather reciprocated. 'Adieu, Julien,' he murmured.

Magalie still clutched Julien's hand and Bob linked arms with Hubert, who held on to Bob's leather vest. The light continued to spread until everything was illuminated. Hubert's eye fell on the two dogs just as their paws were already beginning to fade into nothingness. Then there was nothing but white. The entire universe had been whited out.

Nothing existed. Neither before nor after.

Time had been done away with.

Abruptly, the vineyard was returned to the silence of the night. Far off, a bird called out in alarm.

'Bloody hell!' cried the younger Pierre Chauveau, out of breath, sitting on the ground. He got up and started running through the rows of vines.

His was the only figure moving in the moonlight.

Everything was black. Life consisted only of this sweet, silent darkness, and as he resurfaced it was like coming up from a long dive in a warm sea.

Julien opened his eyes and found himself lying in bed looking at the ceiling of the tiny apartment he had just bought with a twenty-year mortgage at a rate of 1.6 per cent. Without moving, he looked around the room. The decor was unchanged, and he was alone in the bed. He could still feel the touch of Magalie's fingers on his hand but she wasn't there, nor had she ever been. It had only been a dream. He sat on the edge of the bed and picked up his phone from the parquet floor: yes, it was the morning after the night at Hubert's when they had drunk the Château Saint-Antoine. Nothing had happened. The four of them had never gone back to the year the wine was made. He ran his hands through his hair, smiling bitterly at the ridiculousness of it all. He could have sworn he had just heard Mr Flying Saucer saying, 'Adieu, Julien,' as light flooded the vineyard. But no. The black-and-white movie playing inside his head had finished, the word '*Fin*' rolled on screen to the sound of trumpeting music, and that was it, done, no closing credits. The dream had vanished without bothering to wave goodbye.

Julien walked over to the coffee machine, dropped in the capsule and pressed the button, making the whole thing shake.

A pale, frothy stream of coffee trickled out as he went to the table where his computer was still turned on. He pressed a button and the screen lit up to show the document he had been working on the night before. He read through the notes he had been writing for a violet-based cocktail he thought Magalie might like and was thinking of naming 'the Abby'. He took his coffee cup, sat in the armchair and closed his eyes. Julien had to admit he wished he hadn't woken from last night's sleep. It was so disappointing to find that nothing he believed had happened had really taken place – the friendship the four of them had forged, meeting his great-grandfather and, most of all, the night he had spent with Magalie, with the tattoo of the cat under her left breast. And yet it all seemed so real.

The corridors of time, Julien murmured, shaking his head, and just for the fun of it, he picked up the mouse, clicked inside the search box and typed 'Abby Cocktail'.

His computer screen was suddenly filled with hundreds of images of a violet-tinted iridescent short drink served in a Martini glass garnished with a twist of lemon zest cut into the shape of a shooting star. Julien shrank back in his chair and froze for a few seconds. Then he reached out a hesitant hand to click on the first image, which had come from Wikipedia.

Abby

From Wikipedia, the free encyclopedia
The Abby is a cocktail containing gin, vodka, violet syrup and liquorice liqueur, served in a Martini glass garnished with a twist of lemon zest cut into the shape

of a shooting star. It was voted one of the top twenty cocktails of the twentieth century by the Philadelphia Guild of Bartenders in 2010.

History

The Abby was created in 1954 by an unknown bartender at Harry's New York Bar in Paris. It is claimed that the first person to taste the Abby was the actress Audrey Hepburn.

Abby is a diminutive of Abigail. The origin of the drink's name is unknown.

The 267 china fragments of the Eros statue began to tremble ever so slightly, signalling that the tunnel-boring machine was close by. Magalie glanced over at her restorers' diploma hanging in its gold frame on the wall. Yet on this same wall, she had seen shelves of feather dusters made with 'real feathers from happy roosters'. The whole studio had been filled from wall to wall with cleaning products that were no longer available. And pretty young Louise Ménard had offered her coffee while her father read a newspaper report about a flying saucer. She was hoping for a small role in her friend Brigitte's next film. A role she didn't get, or which had gone unnoticed, for no Louise Ménard had left her mark on the seventh art. And so Julien, her neighbour, was nothing more than a fantasy arising out of the impromptu aperitif with Monsieur Larnaudie, whom she had called Hubert in her dream. It was madness to have fallen in love with Julien, who had turned out to be an ideal companion and perfect lover. Everything had been so lovely and easy in the dream, it brought Magalie close to tears.

How on earth could she tell Julien what she had imagined? In the dream, she had gone back to the year the wine was made with Bob the American, Julien and Hubert. She could clearly picture looking down at her boots as she walked along the cobbled Passage Choiseul to visit Odette, and Odette's thirty-one-year-old face was imprinted on her mind more crisply than a digital photograph.

So she was destined to spend the rest of her life fixing broken objects until her hands shook with age. Magalie had an urge to pick up the statue's smiling face and smash it against the table, breaking it into four clean pieces. But she restrained herself and the statue went on smiling blankly at her, as if carrying a silent message. Magalie slipped her hands into the pockets of the strapless dress with the red cat that she had put on again this morning and felt a small, hard-edged object beneath her fingers. An object which, to her expert hand, must be made of wood. She held it up between her thumb and index finger and when she saw it, the walls of the studio began to spin so violently that she staggered backwards and sat in the armchair she normally reserved for her clients.

Julien couldn't tear his eyes off the computer screen and was scrolling through everything he could find about the Abby cocktail when he heard a loud knock at his door. When he opened it, he found Magalie staring back at him.

'Julien,' she murmured, and without another word, she held up the carved figurine of the little grape-picker with his basket.

And they wrapped their arms around one another.

'*Je vouloir un miracle*,' Bob murmured to himself, sitting on his bed, and immediately heard the priest's gentle voice correcting him, '*Je voudrais*'. He had just put his phone down and was staring at the light coming through Madame Renard's curtains. He had been dreaming of being with Magalie, Julien and Hubert in a vineyard where a flying saucer had just flown over, followed by a flash of bright white light, when his phone had rung. For a second he asked himself if extraterrestrials had mobile phone contracts, then he opened his eyes and briefly wondered why he wasn't in Milwaukee. He turned towards the phone on the bedside table, which showed 'Junior' calling and was on its third ring. It was three in the morning in Wisconsin. It must be something serious for his son to be calling in the middle of the night. Bob sat up in bed and picked up the phone, preparing himself to hear the news he had been dreading for months. He would have to hold it together, be brave and not crumble.

'Hello,' he said quietly.

'She woke up!' cried Bob Junior.

'What . . . ?' murmured Bob.

'She woke up!' his son repeated. 'The doctors called us an hour ago. Jenny and I are at the hospital. They've done some tests. She's turned a corner. The blood counts are way up.

They can't understand it. They're saying . . .' His son's voice cracked.

'What are they saying?' asked Bob.

'They're saying it's a miracle,' Junior said breathlessly, and tears ran down Bob's cheeks.

He was now fairly certain that the priest who had heard his plea at Notre-Dame-des-Victoires was God incarnate. If the Church of Miracles really existed, Bob swore that it would soon hold a new marble plaque engraved with the words 'Merci, from Bob Brown, Milwaukee'. Bob opened the curtains. The sky was blue and there was Sacré-Cœur in the distance. He went into the living room and found his stack of three thousand dollars in hundred-dollar bills on the table, with the words 'in God we trust' on the back. He nodded. This morning, he was a believer. He felt suddenly joyful, and opened his palm to look at the broken lifeline. The second half of his existence had started, with Goldie coming back to life. His eye fell on the HOG vest he had carefully hung over the chair the night before. He picked it up, noticing that there were five badges missing, the pin holes still visible in the black leather.

'Everything OK, Monsieur Larnaudie?'

'Everything's just fine, thank you, Maria.'

Madame Da Silva watched from the window of her lodge, a bowl of coffee in her hand. This was the first time she had seen the chairman of the management committee heading for the bins in his dressing gown and slippers, holding a torch. She heard the cellar door bang shut, making her jump. Ten minutes earlier, Hubert had been woken by the buzz of a text message. He had opened his eyes on the familiar decor of his bedroom, sat on the side of his bed and picked up his phone to read: 'Monsieur Van Der Broeck is pleased to confirm your breakfast meeting at 10 a.m. Hotel Meurice – Dalí Suite'. He lay straight back down again. A jumble of images floated inside his head. Images of a train, vines, the original Les Halles, the faces of Jean Gabin and his grandfather André Larnaudie, Abby, Julien, Bob the American, glasses of Bloody Mary at Harry's Bar and German shepherds. Then all these images melded into one: the prettily hand-drawn words LA MAROTTE – COIFFEUR POUR HOMMES ET FEMMES – BARBE ET COUPE arching across the window of a modestly sized hair salon. At the bottom of the window stood a line of gleaming hairdressing trophies. He saw his hand reaching for the doorknob, the door opening with a tinkling bell and everything came back to him.

As Hubert left the living room to go and make a coffee, Mog, the family cat, who had gone into early hibernation on the radiator, briefly opened one eye before resuming his feline dreams. Hubert stopped in front of the portrait of Anatole and looked into the piercing eyes, perfectly captured by the long-suffering anonymous artist for whom the old curmudgeon had sat a century earlier. 'Have you never wondered how Anatole was able to pay for a lift in 1911 out of his own pocket?' Hubert knotted his dressing gown, took the keys to the cellar and a torch from a drawer in the hallway and slammed the door behind him.

As he made his way downstairs, he was increasingly aware that he was embarking on a ridiculous enterprise. Turning the corner in the underground corridor, he noticed the crowbar marks on Madame Merlino's and Monsieur Berthier's doors. He carried on to his own cellar and turned the key in the door. He unceremoniously pushed aside all the clutter from the room where he had found the bottle of Château Saint-Antoine 1954: the candelabra, the bedside table, the stacks of *L'Illustration*, the old rolled-up posters and eighteenth-century engravings. He reached for the shovel that had tripped him the day before and began to bang it against the dirt floor to the left of the former coal bunker, when he was startled to hear a hollow sound. He scraped the shovel across the ground until a square outline was revealed. He carried on and a cast-iron ring appeared. Hubert was surprised to hear himself let out a high-pitched chuckle as he knelt down. He sneezed, put two fingers inside the metal ring and pulled with all his might. The trapdoor opened in a cloud of dust, revealing a flight of stairs leading down into the darkness. Hubert sat, stunned, for a few seconds, then he raced across the room to slam the door closed and returned to the hole in the ground. He turned on the torch and cautiously began to descend.

Stone steps going down ten yards and a second, smaller staircase that goes deeper still, Léonard had said. It was silent at first and there was a strong smell of damp from the old stones.

'Anatole . . .' Hubert whispered as he descended into the depths of 18 Rue Edgar-Charellier.

When he reached the bottom of the first set of steps, he could hear a distant whirring noise, but he paid little attention as he made his way down the second staircase, more cramped than the first. The torchlight illuminated the narrow steps spiralling down into the darkness. He was already picturing himself heading into the crypt, kneeling in front of one of the three enormous chests and lifting the heavy steel lid to find gold coins, silver ciboria and ruby- and emerald-encrusted crosses. 'It would take four men to carry one of those chests,' Léonard had said, and Hubert wondered if there would be enough to allow him to buy back the whole building and reinstate Anatole's empire. He would begin by acquiring Léonard's apartment, now in the hands of the Ménards, and doing as his grandfather never had – knocking it through into his own flat. He would pay above the going rate to get the Ménards out as quickly as possible, and then he would have the fireplaces put back. Next he would buy the apartment above to make a duplex. Then the one below. He would only keep Abby and Julien in the building. And Bob. He would buy the studio from Madame Renard and give it to him in the name of Franco-American friendship.

'The monks' gold . . .' he whispered.

Silent men hiding a lust for wealth under their habits had accumulated all of this for the Larnaudies, so that one of them would find it one day. A kind of reward, a justification for having erected the building under Baron Haussmann.

At the bottom of the steps, the whirring sound was much clearer. Hubert stepped into the large, empty room in front of him and banged his head against a pillar, causing him to stagger backwards and see luminous butterflies dancing before his eyes. The whirring sound grew louder, but he couldn't tell if it was real or inside his head. He shone his torch around the walls, looking for the entrance to the corridor leading to the crypt. The beam of light picked out an opening large enough for a man to step through. Hubert hurried over and, as he went inside, the noise intensified and he thought he could see a glimmer of light at the end of the tunnel. How could there be light in a crypt no one had set foot in since the 1930s? Hubert crept further down the corridor. Now the whirring was accompanied by sounds of water and engines running. He also thought he heard voices. At the end of the tunnel, he was blinded by a bright white light like the flash of the flying saucer, and noise filled his ears.

Shielding his eyes with one hand, he found himself looking at an enormous building site. Here, underground, dozens of men were working under bright lights inside a giant tubular concrete bunker, building something out of science fiction: the extension of metro line 14. The tunnel-boring machine, which looked like a wingless Boeing with a boring wheel on its head, was moving forward to the clamour of pistons and spraying water. Hubert was standing just inside the corridor when the workers looked up and saw him.

'Hey, Monsieur!' a man in overalls and a hard hat shouted. 'You're not allowed down here. Go and get Martinez,' he told a colleague.

Hubert looked at him, wild-eyed.

'But . . . the crypt,' he muttered. 'You've destroyed the crypt. It was right here!' he cried, pointing to the tunnel the machine had bored. 'Here!' he said again, on the verge of either a breakdown or a heart attack. 'You've drilled through everything!'

'What the hell's this guy in a dressing gown doing in my tunnel?' muttered the site manager, bemused, as he was led towards Hubert. 'How did you get here?!' he shouted.

'Through my cellar!' Hubert replied.

'Through his cellar,' the manager repeated, stunned. 'Never in my life . . . In thirty years of construction, I've never seen this before. You need to go back to your cellar and go home. And fast – we're about to close it all up.'

'Boss!' a man called from the tunnel-boring machine and the site manager headed towards him, shouting over to a tall man who was looking at Hubert, 'Get him to go home!'

'There was treasure here,' Hubert said flatly as he stared into the tunnel.

The worker stepped towards him and said softly, 'There's no such thing as treasure.'

Hubert looked up at him.

'The treasure is you, you in your own home – do you see?' he said, placing a hand on Hubert's shoulder. 'The treasure is life. It's looking at the blue sky from your balcony. That is the only treasure.'

Hubert stared at him for some time before nodding and closing his eyes.

'I'm sure you're right,' he said weakly, placing his hand on his shoulder.

'Trust me.' The man shook his head. 'Go back home. Think of me down here and look up at the sky for me.'

Hubert agreed, heading back into the corridor and disappearing into the gloom, raising his hand in farewell.

Magalie, Julien and Bob kept banging on Hubert's door, but he still didn't answer. They were beginning to wonder whether he had been left behind in 1954, when the lift stopped and there he was in his dressing gown, covered in dust, with a torch in his hand.

'Where have you been?' Julien asked.

'You'll never believe me,' moaned Hubert.

'It wasn't a dream, Hubert,' Magalie said gravely.

'Oh, I know,' he sighed. 'I almost wish it had been. Come in and have coffee.'

As they went into the kitchen, Hubert told himself that perhaps the wall between his apartment and Léonard's would no longer be standing. André Larnaudie might have followed his advice and cashed in his shares in the Suez Canal, avoiding bankruptcy and having to sell his missing cousin's apartment off cheap. But no, the kitchen was as he had always known it and the empty bottle of Château Saint-Antoine 1954, Domaine Jules Beauchamps, stood on the counter. They all looked at it and then at each other.

'Hug, Hubert,' said Bob, throwing his arms around Hubert, and Magalie and Julien joined them, the four of them reunited after all their adventures.

As they drank their coffee, Bob told them about the phone call from his son and how Goldie had woken up and was in remission, which he put down to his visit to Notre-Dame-des-Victoires.

'To Goldie,' said Hubert, raising his coffee cup.

'To Goldie,' Magalie and Julien echoed.

'To the two of you,' said Bob, 'who've found love, which is what matters most.'

Then they all turned to Hubert questioningly.

'Me?' He walked over to the kitchen window and threw it open on the courtyard. 'I found the blue sky,' he said, gazing up above the zinc roofs of Paris.

Far from 18 Rue Edgar-Charellier, in Charmally-les-Vignes in the year 1978, Pierre Chauveau, known as Mr Flying Saucer, was woken by his wife flinging open the bedroom door.

'Get up and come and see this!' she cried. 'There's another dog in the courtyard, grey like a wolf. It's as if Sieg had come back to life!'

At that moment, the two dogs pushed past her and positioned themselves either side of the bed. Pierre yawned, plumped his pillow behind his head and took off his nightcap.

'You know,' he smiled. 'Life is full of mysteries, Mélanie dear. And if you'd like to warm us up some coffee, I'll tell you a story we could call "the Saint-Antoine mystery". Isn't that right, boy?' he said, nodding at his four-legged friend.

And the Alsatian barked twice.

I would like to thank, in order of appearance, however fleeting:

HRH The Duke of Windsor, Salvador Dalí, Jacques Prévert, Robert Doisneau, Marcel Aymé, Harry MacElhone, François Truffaut, Claude Chabrol, Jean-Luc Godard, Audrey Hepburn, Hubert de Givenchy, Jean Gabin and Édith Piaf.

Thanks to Laurent Giraud-Dumas at Harry's New York Bar for answering all my questions and creating 'the Abby' especially for this book. Thanks to Hervé Lorin for sharing his knowledge of Beaujolais Nouveau. Thanks to Sophie Jehan for having, however unwittingly, given me the idea for Magalie's career, for which her own provided the inspiration. Thanks to my American friends in Milwaukee, Wisconsin, particularly Daniel Goldin and his team at Boswell Book Company. Thanks to Liam Callanan and to Jim Fricke, Curatorial Director of the Harley-Davidson Museum, for letting me into the archives and workshops. Thanks to the aircraft pilots – civil and military – who all told me they had seen 'strange things' in the sky during their careers. Thanks to Jean Castelli, who has read the manuscripts of all my books, for confirming that the capital and Les Halles in 1954 as I describe them in this book correspond to the Paris he knew.

Reading Group Questions

- To what extent does Antoine Laurain paint a nostalgic picture of 1950s France?

- What does the journey back in time teach the four about life in the 1950s? How does it make them see their lives in the present day differently? Which character do you think learns the most from the experience?

- Back in 1954, the characters cannot reach for their mobile phones to look things up or contact their friends. What does the novel have to say about our reliance on technology?

- 'Great novels are above all great fairytales,' said Vladimir Nabokov. Is *Vintage 1954* a fairytale? If so, is there a moral of the story?

- Antoine Laurain has flirted with the fantastic in past novels – Mitterrand's homburg in *The President's Hat* and the painting in *The Portrait* may or may not have possessed magical properties. Does the time travel in *Vintage 1954* move this novel into a different realm?

- Antoine Laurain began his career as an assistant to an antique dealer. Antiques and objects often feature prominently in his novels. What is the significance of objects in *Vintage 1954*, and of Magalie's profession as an antique restorer?

- Is Antoine Laurain an optimistic writer? Can his novels, and other recent 'uplifting' reads, be seen as a reaction to the turbulent times we are living in?

The President's Hat

Antoine Laurain

Translated by Jane Aitken, Emily Boyce and
Louise Rogers Lalaurie

'A hymn to *la vie Parisienne* . . . enjoy it for its fabulistic
narrative, and the way it teeters pleasantly on the edge of
Gallic whimsy' Paperback of the Week, *The Guardian*

Dining alone in an elegant Parisian brasserie, accountant
Daniel Mercier can hardly believe his eyes when President
François Mitterrand sits down to eat at the table next to him.

Daniel's thrill at being in such close proximity to the
most powerful man in the land persists even after the
presidential party has gone, which is when he discovers
that Mitterrand's black felt hat has been left behind.

After a few moments' soul-searching, Daniel decides to
keep the hat as a souvenir of an extraordinary evening. It's
a perfect fit, and as he leaves the restaurant Daniel begins
to feel somehow . . . different.

ISBN: 9781908313478
e-ISBN: 9781908313577

The Red Notebook

Antoine Laurain

Translated by Jane Aitken and Emily Boyce

'In equal parts an offbeat romance, detective story and
a clarion call for metropolitans to look after their
neighbours . . . Reading *The Red Notebook* is a little
like finding a gem among the bric-a-brac in a local *brocante*'
Christian House, *The Telegraph*

'Resist this novel if you can; it's the very quintessence of
French romance' *The Times*

Bookseller Laurent Letellier comes across an abandoned
handbag on a Parisian street, and feels impelled to return
it to its owner.

The bag contains no money, phone or contact information.
But a small red notebook with handwritten thoughts
and jottings reveals a person that Laurent would very
much like to meet.

Without even a name to go on, and only a few of her
possessions to help him, how is he to find one woman in
a city of millions?

ISBN: 9781908313867
e-ISBN: 9781908313874

French Rhapsody

Antoine Laurain

Translated by Jane Aitken and Emily Boyce

'Beautifully written, superbly plotted and with a brilliant twist at the end' *Daily Mail*

'The novel has Laurain's signature charm, but with the added edge of greater engagement with contemporary France ' *Sunday Times*

Middle-aged doctor Alain Massoulier has received a life-changing letter – thirty-three years too late. Lost in the Paris postal system for decades, the letter from Polydor, dated 1983, offers a recording contract to The Holograms, in which Alain played lead guitar. Overcome by nostalgia, Alain is tempted to track down the members of the group. But in a world where everything and everyone has changed . . . where could his quest possibly take him?

Both a modern fairytale and a skilfully woven state-of-the-nation novel, *French Rhapsody* combines Antoine Laurain's signature charm and whimsy with a searing critique of the state of contemporary France.

ISBN: 9781910477304
e-ISBN: 9781910477380

The Portrait

Antoine Laurain

Translated by Jane Aitken and Emily Boyce

'A delightful literary soufflé that fans of his other charming books will savor.' *Library Journal*

While wandering through a Paris auction house, avid collector Pierre-François Chaumont is stunned to discover the eighteenth-century portrait of an unknown man who looks just like him.

Much to his delight, Chaumont's bid for the work is successful, but back at home his jaded wife and circle of friends are unable to see the resemblance.

Chaumont remains convinced of it, and as he researches into the painting's history, he is presented with the opportunity to abandon his tedious existence and walk into a brand new life . . .

ISBN: 9781910477434
e-ISBN: 9781910477458

Smoking Kills

Antoine Laurain

Translated by Louise Rogers Lalaurie

'Funny, superbly over-the-top . . . not a page too much'
The Times

'Hilarious . . . *formidable* – and essential packing for
any French summer holiday' *Daily Mail*

When head-hunter Fabrice Valentine faces a smoking ban
at work, he decides to undertake a course of hypnotherapy
to rid himself of the habit. At first the treatment works,
but his stress levels begin to rise when he is passed over for
an important promotion and he finds himself lighting up
again – but with none of his previous enjoyment.

Until he discovers something terrible: he accidentally
causes a man's death, and needing a cigarette to calm
his nerves, he enjoys it more than any other previous
smoke. What if he now needs to kill every time he wants
to properly appreciate his next Benson and Hedges?

ISBN: 9781910477540
e-ISBN: 9781910477557